Slippery when wet

Martin Goodman

Other titles published by transita

transita

To find out more about transita, our books and our authors visit
www.transita.co.uk

Slippery when wet

Martin Goodman

transita

Published by Transita
3 Newtec Place, Magdalen Road,
Oxford OX4 1RE. United Kingdom.
Tel: (01865) 204393. Fax: (01865) 248780.
email: info@transita.co.uk
http://www.transita.co.uk

British Library Cataloguing in Publication Data
A catalogue record for this book is available from the British Library

Cover design by Baseline Arts Ltd, Oxford
Produced for Transita by Deer Park Productions, Tavistock
Typeset by PDQ Typesetting, Newcastle-under-Lyme
Printed and bound by Bookmarque, Croydon

ABOUT THE AUTHOR

Martin Goodman's first novel was shortlisted for the Whitbread Award. The Los Angeles Times wrote of him: 'Such narrow, narrow confines we live in. Every so often, one of us primates escapes these dimensions, as Martin Goodman did. All we can do is rattle the bars and look after him as he runs into the hills. We wait for his letters home.' After years of pushing non-fiction to its limits, writing books and feature articles that tell true stories from the wild side of life, *Slippery When Wet* marks his return to the novel. The book emerges from a lifetime of rubbing Englishness against the edge of different civilizations: Martin has worked in China, Saudi Arabia, Thailand, Holland, Germany, Italy and Qatar, and has homes in England, Santa Fe (New Mexico), and the French Pyrenees. This book was written as a sixtieth birthday present for a very special lady, to prove that a fine vintage blends youth with experience.

ACKNOWLEDGEMENTS

The Scottish Arts Council awarded me a travel bursary, which paid for one of my research trips to Bangladesh, a vital element in the making of this book. World Vision arranged for me to visit several of their projects in Bangladesh. Many folk in Bangladesh were exceptionally gracious and open in sharing their country with me.

Greg Wise accompanied me on my trip out to Kanachanburi, where I garnered material for the River Kwai element of the book.

Tom Christie has sustained this book with his belief, shaping it with expert editorial comments.

Nikki Read, Giles Lewis and Fiona Davis at Transita have given this book a happy sense of coming home.

Ben Mason at Sheil Land has taken the book under his wing.

James Thornton has filtered this book through countless hundreds of pages, with his kind, judicious, and miraculously persistent editorial eye.

My heartfelt thanks to one and all.

DEDICATION

For Kay O'Neill
Whose book this is

PART ONE

Mawsby Hall

Spring 1992

CHAPTER 1

THUNDER CRASHED THROUGH THE CHAMBERS of the stately home, cradling Maggie's four-poster within its sound. As rains lashed the windows and coated the sweep of lawns, she didn't wake.

The tip of her tongue moistened her lips though, which then smiled.

She felt sexy in her dreams.

* * *

Maggie's telephone was hooked to a private line. She gave the number to nobody. The instrument, a large black Bakelite, squatted on her bedside table.

Its ring was loud. Down pillows absorbed the jerk of her head as she jolted awake. She knocked the receiver off the hook, then picked it up to lay it on the pillow beside her ear.

'Hello,' a voice said. A thin voice of a woman.

Maggie felt no urge to respond.

'Mrs Mawsby?' the thin voice squeaked, both proud and scared to be so demanding. A village woman. Maggie knew the type. 'I know you're there, Mrs Mawsby. I can hear you breathing. This is Miss Dirkin. Angela Dirkin. I've got your husband here.'

Wherever her husband was, it was no news to Maggie. News has to be interesting. She was not interested in her husband.

'Your husband, Mrs Mawsby. He's with me. He's in my bed.'

Maggie let the silence reign so long, she realised it was her turn to speak.

'What do you want? Congratulations or sympathy?'

'He's dead, Mrs Mawsby. Chumpers is dead.'

'Chumpers?' Maggie snorted, gripped the phone, and started to sit up. How absurd that he should let a village woman use his pet name.

'You're laughing, Mrs Mawsby. Laughing at your husband's death.'

'No, my dear.' It was too early to banter etiquette with the village slut. Time to gather the facts and conclude the conversation. 'So Charles has died?'

'In the night.'

'When, exactly?'

'There was a storm. A crack of thunder. I think it shocked him.'

Maggie looked through her bedroom window. The sky was blue, yet so clear that the news of a storm in the night made sense. The day had been washed clean.

'You must come around, Mrs Mawsby. Come and collect him. His body can't be discovered here. It simply wouldn't do.'

Maggie would not tolerate being told what to do by such a woman. She replaced the receiver. Then took it off its hook so it would not ring again.

* * *

4

This was a rare morning worth leaving bed to discover. Rain perfumed the air. Maggie walked the driveway breathing in scents from the trees. It was years since she'd come this way on foot. Normally she used the Peugeot runabout for brief excursions into the village. Windows up, doors locked, engine running, she was glad of the protection of the car's tin casing. If people waved she nodded in response, like a nervous tick, and kept both hands on the wheel. She was used to winding the car around the small pits in the driveway. Now the broken surface pressed through the soles of her feet and she felt connected. Weeds had pierced the thin spikes of new leaves through the asphalt. How brave. How reckless we are, to think we can ever hold back nature.

She didn't stop at the front gate, pillars topped with real cannonballs edging the mass of wrought iron that always stood open nowadays, but continued straight out of the estate. The grass on the far side of the road was long. It licked itself around her legs and soaked her shoes. She walked through it as far as the stream. Its waters ran fast. She stood for some minutes then walked upstream. It was good to be moving beside the flow. The rush of its energy filled her.

The toe of her right shoe caught against the ground.

She kicked with her toes to unearth a stick. Its bark was dark and shiny. Taking hold of its cloven end, she ran her fingers around its smooth tip. It made her laugh. Poor, silly, phallic stick.

With a gentle swing of her arm she threw it into the stream.

It leapt like a salmon then darted forward like a pike, its sudden vigour surprising her. She found herself running to keep up, till it became stuck behind some rocks where it whirled around and around.

Out on the country road a car ground into low gear to take a bend.

Crows cawed and cackled into flight, a grating sound that chased across the morning.

The car backfired.

Maggie jumped at the noise. She turned from the stream to look down the road. Her granddaughter's yellow Mini came into view. Climbing from the grass of the verge Maggie intercepted the car before it could turn in through the gates.

'Good morning, Flick,' she said, as the girl wound down her window.

The girl's hair was lank, as though wet. Her eyes blinked round and slow within the circle of her face.

Maggie watched her mouth open to speak.

My granddaughter's like a creature of the sea, she thought. A creature of the sea bed. Her yellow car is a shell she has outgrown. She needs to leave it for something larger.

'What are you doing out here, Gran?'

Maggie watched the mouth move, without listening to the words. She pressed the button on the handle and pulled the car door open.

'Come on out, Flick. I've got something to show you.'

The girl swelled out of the car while her grandmother stepped back.

'Let me take you for a little walk.' Maggie led the way. 'You must still be dull from your London, Flick. Breathe as we go. Smell the earth. The sky fell down on it last night. It's excited. Come and see what the storm has done to the stream.'

They walked the road, then cut in to where Maggie had found the stick.

'There was a stick,' she said. 'Caught in the ground, just here. It made me laugh. Looked like a black man's penis. I picked it up and threw it in...'

She mirrored the stick's flight with her hand, and spread her fingers wide to show how it splashed into the stream. Her hand then pointed out the stick's route as she led the way along the bank.

'It tore itself from the clutches of those weeds...' she told, and heard the drama in her voice. A tale told with such effect needed an ending. She hoped she could find one. '.... knocked against the roots of that tree... span off between the stones... surged along this straight bit thinking all was going well... then tumbled down the waterfall.'

The stream was full, but it was just a stream. Flick ambled along, taking one step to every two of her grandmother's, and wondered what the fuss was about. The 'waterfall' was only six inches deep. Then they came upon the stick.

It was about a foot long, one end slightly forked like a fish's tail. It had dropped into a small pool, a whirl of water behind rocks that took up a narrow section of the stream. The stick kept spiralling round, racing an ever broader circle till it seemed about to be flung free. The end reached out of the whirlpool, closer and closer to a boulder that stood at its side. Then one brief tap, wood upon stone, and the stick was tipped from the edge and sucked back into the centre.

With nothing else to point to, Maggie let her hands drop to her sides.

'It's just a stick,' she said.

Flick knew as much. Her grandmother's excitement puzzled her, but that her story simply tailed off was no surprise. Flick found people's excitement often evaporated in her company.

'Don't you see, it's just a stick,' Maggie insisted, and her excitement was back. In this simple fact her story had found its conclusion at last. 'I thought it had the secret at first. I watched it go with the flow. But it's only a stick. It's been caught up like that for an hour now.'

They watched it get knocked back from a few more escape attempts.

'Look and learn, Flick. Look and learn. People tell us nowadays that we should go with the flow. This is proof that going with the flow is not enough. That stick needs arms. And maybe legs. It needs to be able to kick out on its own.'

Maggie turned from the scene, tired of it suddenly, and stepped back to the road.

'Sometimes it requires an effort of our own. If we're not to get stuck.'

A tractor had been working out of sight. Now it carried its noise over the hill, and drew fresh lines with its plough as it drove toward them. A white band of seagulls streamed out in its wake, brilliant against the brown.

'Stupid birds!' Maggie was dazzled by the sight, but turned away in annoyance. 'They've got webbed feet yet they paddle about the countryside.'

'The plough's turning up food for them,' Flick explained. 'Worms and things.'

Maggie regarded the girl.

'I know what the birds are doing,' she said. 'They're searching for scraps. When all the oceans could be theirs, I simply wonder why.'

Flick looked at her grandmother, and saw tears seep from her eyes.

'What's the matter?' she asked. 'Is something wrong?'

Maggie blinked back her response. After an absence, the sight of her granddaughter always stupefied her. She felt herself shrink before the girl's size. She once tried to understand the phenomenon by imagining an acorn being filled with earth, first by the pinch and then the shovel-full, thrusting itself downwards and upwards as roots and branches till it was filled out as an oak tree.

'It's your grandfather,' she said. 'He's left me.'

'Left you?'

'In the night. I had a call. Your grandfather's dead.'

The girl gaped.

'I'm off there now. Off to see him.'

Maggie started to walk.

'How?' Flick asked as she hurried to catch up. 'How did it happen?'

'Happen? Death just happens. We do what we can then death takes over.'

She let the thought hang around her for a moment, then took hold of her skirt by its pleats and held it out to the sides. It had hidden in her closet for years. The dress was pleasantly loose about her neck and gathered in folds around her body. The folds dropped extra patterns of light and shadow upon the material, a dark blue silk which swished above her skin when she moved.

It was fun to walk in.

'I'll walk, if you don't mind. You can follow me in your little car.'

'Back up to the house?'

Flick could see through the gates to a distant corner of Mawsby Hall, standing at an angle to the avenue of trees.

Maggie kept her back to the sight.

'Oh no.' The words were spoken quietly as Maggie's head shivered from side to side. 'Your grandfather's in the village. The first house on the left. I'll see you there.'

Maggie tried to give the girl a smile, but didn't know if it showed. She felt nothing of it herself but its ache in her cheeks.

Flick watched the woman turn. The dress was askew on her shoulders, narrow shoulders with skin that was close to the bone. The white strands of the woman's hair were pinned to her scalp by combs, as though fixed while being blown in a high wind. It left her neck bare, and her ears sticking out like a lamb's.

Flick watched the figure walk the country road till it grew tiny, then climbed into her car and followed.

CHAPTER 2

L aid flat around the end-terraced cottage, the garden made no concession to spring.

Maggie approved.

There was no silly seasonal show of colour, tulips and daffodils waving about on insipid stems. Simply the soil turned, the lawn trimmed, and the roses pruned to stubs. It was a garden where winter had been, with space for summer to come if it so chose.

The upstairs window was open. Grunts and sighs and the creaking of wood came from inside.

Maggie didn't pause to feel curious, but strode up the path and opened the front door. The staircase led up like a boxed-in ladder from the tiny square of the hallway. Maggie took hold of the handrail and climbed out of Flick's sight.

There was nothing for Flick to do but follow. The noises from inside the bedroom stopped as she climbed the stairs.

Maggie had stationed herself just inside the door, while a woman stood to the left at the far side of a double bed.

Flick paused in the doorway.

'Hello,' the woman said.

Her round face was held between wads of hair that were like wire pot scourers, and she stared through thick-rimmed glasses. Below her Flick's grandfather lay naked on the bed. His flesh was speckled. His stomach looked pregnant.

'You must be the granddaughter,' the woman announced. 'I'm Angela Dirkin.'

She raised her right hand, then sliced it as a karate chop into the dead man's stomach. It pushed out a scrap of air that made his soft lips flutter.

Angela reached round his left shoulder to heave him upright and hold him sitting for a moment. Then the support was taken away and his head fell back into its pillows.

Moving round the bed, Angela climbed up to join him. She knelt with her back to Flick, took hold of the man's left foot, then pushed till the kneecap was pressed in close to his chest.

'What are you doing?' Flick asked.

The foot was raised till its toes pointed to the ceiling, then the leg slammed back to the mattress.

'Can I help?'

'Help?'

Angela laughed into the word. She kept her back to Flick, the shoulders shaking in the black-ribbed sweater.

'Oh no. Angela Dirkin goes it alone. She's got hours left in her yet.'

She picked up the man's leg by its foot and bounced it a few times. Flick hurried forward and laid a hand on one of the woman's shoulders. Angela toppled sideways into her arms, forcing the girl onto the bed. The woman's laughter turned to damp sobs which she pressed in between Flick's breasts.

Flick kept her hands on the bed to support them both while Angela did the hugging. The sobs draw back into gasps and then silence.

'So this is it,' Maggie said, aloud but to herself. 'This is the end.'

* * *

The end had been a long time coming.

Maggie had guessed at it from the very beginning. She was a teenager visiting Mawsby Hall when Charles, the son and heir, returned from the war. The war for her largely consisted of supplementing rations with rabbits caught in traps. Their squeals pierced through radio broadcasts of news from the front. She would go out and club the creatures' heads, then work their feet free of spiked iron clamps with some tenderness. That was how she spent her nights. In the daytime she sometimes tracked squads of Home Guard on field exercises. It helped her imagine the lives of real soldiers out there on the world's frontlines.

When Charles Mawsby got out of the car, she recognised her imagination was just a silly thing. It had taught her nothing about the effects of frontline combat.

This young man reeked of war. It had aged him to the verge of death. His family wept and hugged him close, but soon let go. His body was brittle and felt breakable. He had nothing to give in return. His eyes shed no tears. His childhood home found no reflection in them. They were dead eyes. Any life he had was hidden far behind them.

Years later Maggie read a serious book that told of the conditioning of women. It claimed they were trained to wait for the moment at which they could sacrifice themselves. The book continued to show women the way to step beyond self-sacrifice, but Maggie did not read that far. She threw the book away.

The return of Charles Mawsby was that sacrificial moment in her life.

She chose to die that he might live. Their eventual marriage was her act of charity. She sat up on their wedding night and watched his body in sleep. It lay as passive as the earth, but a patch of the earth with a fault-line running beneath it. Some day it would quake, and life would change.

She knew this then. It was her core knowledge as a young bride. As the decades passed it grew dim, but the knowledge was still there. And waiting.

* * *

The body before her now was old and flabby, but the stick of the man she married was buried somewhere within it. Much of his sandy hair had drifted away. Under his belly his penis peeked through a knot of grey hairs like a vole from its grassy hole. He was circumcised as a baby. She let her imagination run through the operation when her own baby son was born, and cried. In due course, her son's foreskin was spared.

She walked up to the bed, laid her hands upon the speckled flesh of her husband's stomach, and felt its waves move beneath her touch. Her hands were sweaty and stuck there but the stomach was cool.

'You can smile, Mrs Mawsby,' Angela Dirkin said.

It was a surprise to Maggie to hear she was smiling. She must have gone off into a reverie.

'You should have come two hours ago. You didn't see it. There was filth. Filth like I'm sure you've never seen. Thank God I had this plastic sheet on the mattress.'

The sheet crinkled beneath Angela's knees as she sat back on her heels. Maggie looked down at it. The plastic was tinted pink and gave a sheen to the floral pattern beneath. Her husband was lying on a bed of roses.

'You wouldn't think a body could make such a mess of itself. It was covered, Mrs Mawsby. Covered in... shit.'

Angela had paused before saying her rude word. A blush bloomed on her cheeks.

'The sheets are in the bathtub. I put them in to soak, and brought up the bucket and floorcloth to wipe him clean. Then sponged down the sheet and dried him off. You're all right now, Mrs Mawsby. It's all right for you to touch him now. Someone else has done the dirty work.'

Maggie considered what to say.

'You're very kind,' she decided.

'It's not kindness. It's duty. Doing what has to be done. And we're not finished yet. He isn't dressed.'

'We could leave if you'd like to play some more.'

'Play?'

'You were hauling his naked body about. Limb by limb.'

'Oh Mrs Mawsby...' Maggie watched Angela's slack-jawed face screw up till its mouth was a walnut, then spring open again. 'You've a nasty mind. I've worked, how I've worked, pumping and twisting him so he wouldn't stiffen up. So you wouldn't have the shame of having your husband found dead in someone else's bed. So no one need know. Locked in rigor mortis, that's how he'd be if I hadn't done my best. How would you fold him up and put him in your car then?'

Maggie used to laugh at the bizarre questions of the villagers. Lately she had been meeting them with silence.

'You wouldn't get far, would you?' Angela persisted.

Maggie wasn't listening. She had started to explore the room.

The carpet first. It was a light tan with a narrow crimson border, its design dense but also intricate, a scattering of miniature leaves that might have blown off a paisley pattern. Maggie crouched and stroked a hand across it.

'How beautiful it is. And I haven't missed it for years.' She looked up at Flick. 'This used to be in the library. The books there are dull, but I liked reading the pattern in the carpet.'

She traced the carpet's threads with her fingertips, then turned to face Angela.

'Well, I hope you had some fun on it,' she said.

Maggie continued to an oak chest of drawers. On top of it a pine marten had risen onto its hind legs, sniffing the scent of dead moss within its glass case. Nearby a grouse ran toward it, trapped beneath a glass bubble and racing forever over its tuft of moorland.

Maggie turned around. Just above Angela's new position a badger's head peered out from a shield on the wall.

16

'Charles always cared for stuffed animals,' Maggie remembered. 'It was the child in him. You've been kind to indulge him, Miss Dirkin. This couldn't have been to your taste. You'll be glad to clear it all out.'

'Oh no, Mrs Mawsby.' Angela raised a finger and waved it from side to side. 'He said you were clever, too clever for him, but that doesn't make me stupid. I'm not soft, Mrs Mawsby. I'm not going to stand here and let you walk off with whatever takes your fancy. Nothing leaves this room unless it's dispatched by me, Mrs Mawsby. Do you hear me? Nothing.'

'Nothing?' Maggie raised an eyebrow, and turned her head to face her husband's body.

'You know what I mean.' Angela clenched her wagging finger within her hand. 'You know I don't mean that. You've got to take him away. He can't be found here. It wouldn't do.'

This room was Charles's secret place. It betrayed the scope of his ambitions. He installed Maggie in his ancestral home but maintained this little space for his own comfort. The browns and beiges, the dim light from the single window, the stuffed animals, it had the air of some chamber in a Victorian museum.

The room was choked with his dead man's breath, arranged in layers like old blankets. It was time to get out.

'Let's be having you,' Maggie said, and picked up the underpants to hook over his toes. The underpants were white but a yellow stain smeared the loose pouch in the front. By lifting one of his feet at a time she worked them past his ankles then up over his kneecaps and onto his thighs.

'Time to help me now, Charles,' she said, and prepared to slide her hands under his backside to lift him a little. 'Shift yourself.'

He wouldn't budge, he wouldn't roll. Maggie kept to her task till both her hands had burrowed beneath his flesh, and there they stuck. She couldn't lift, she couldn't pull. Her hands were caught between the man's right buttock and the mattress.

'Let go,' she insisted, and closed her eyes to wish herself free. 'You're sitting on me. Let go.'

He didn't respond. Hadn't for years. Death had changed nothing there.

She yanked her hands free. Her sorry hands. She held them out to recover, palms spread flat about a foot above the dead man's stomach. An ache was wrapped around them like bandages, or ectoplasm, something she could see through. The hands themselves looked small within the hurt, the fingers shivering, the backs mottled brown. Like trout, she thought. My hands are like trout, swimming against a stream.

Angela approached the bed. The underpants had been drawn into a narrow band to bind the man's thighs. She hooked in her thumbs. The man's waist flew high at the touch. With a couple of bounces the pants were on.

Maggie admired the touch. It was nicely British. Firm and vigorous, an attempt after decency where it could be of little help.

* * *

18

Maggie carried her husband's jacket downstairs and into the garden. She wanted to examine the wallet in the inside jacket pocket.

She had given it to Charles for his sixtieth birthday. He was now seventy-two. The black leather had faded and the brass trimmings come adrift. Maggie spread the jacket on the lawn as a seat, sat with her legs half-crossed, and took out the money.

There were two hundred and seventy pounds. She counted it more out of habit than interest, and held the credit cards up so that the sunlight played rainbows across their laser logos. Then she explored further. Two black and white photographs slid out from an inside pocket.

The first was of a young woman. Herself. She wore a fresh-faced smile, a pleated dress, a coronet of braided hair, and was standing on the forecourt of Mawsby Hall, soon after she was installed as its mistress.

The other photo was taken in a place where she had never been.

It showed six men standing in a line. Their arms linked one another's shoulders. They were naked but for triangular cloths that covered their groins and were knotted at their waists by strings. Their bodies were tanned, and in the gloss of the photo their skins shone. The flesh of each man was patterned with the bones of his skeleton. Two of the men had shaved heads, the others ragged cuts, but they were all clean shaven. Their feet stood on dust. At an angle behind them was a long thatched hut. Except for small patches of sky the rest of the background was made up of trees.

Charles was the second from the left. He looked the same age as the others. Somewhere in his late sixties.

He was in fact twenty-three. So were the others, more or less.

Maggie was eleven at the time the photo was taken. She went that year to see the film of *The Jungle Book*. It was shot just outside Los Angeles, and its version of India convinced her. The first passion of her awakening sexual life was the sleek-limbed young boy who played Mowgli.

Years later she went to the cinema with Charles to see *The Bridge on the River Kwai*. He gripped both armrests tight throughout the film. When they got home he fetched out this little photograph.

'The film looked beautiful,' he said. 'The light, the music, the actors. But look at us!'

He stabbed a finger at the picture and his row of friends. 'Death on sticks.'

It was the legs that were like sticks. And the flesh was sucked from the bodies.

Maggie opened her eyes in the garden and looked at the picture again.

'Why don't you go back?' she had suggested to Charles just the year before. 'I'll come too.'

A travel brochure had come through the post and she had opened it on Thailand. One packaged holiday combined a week on a beach, some days in Bangkok, and a visit to the River Kwai. She pointed to the inset photograph of the bridge across the river. Charles glanced at it, then turned his head away and stepped back from the table.

'It's not a place,' he said. 'It's a time. There's no going back.'

'You could take me.'

'It would mean a bus trip. You know I don't like buses.'

'A man who built a railroad can survive a bus trip.'

'I wouldn't.'

'Then you can die on the bus. We'll bury you in the jungle with your friends. That would suit you, wouldn't it?' She tore the page from the travel brochure and waved it at him. 'You never came back from that jungle. That's what I think. I'm your wife but I've never known you. Never known you come alive. I married a corpse. Let's take you back and bury you. That's what women do who marry corpses. It sets them free.'

Now he was truly dead. She slid the photograph back into the wallet and stood up. There was a dark wet patch on the lining of the jacket. Water had soaked through from the lawn, reaching through the silk of her skirt to touch cold against her skin. She picked the jacket up to see how much it was ruined, then realised it didn't matter.

There was a noise from the house.

Angela was holding the front door open while the figure of Flick came down the last steps of the staircase. Maggie saw the head of her husband nodding slowly, his chin bouncing upon the crown of Flick's head, one arm draped across each of her shoulders, his legs scissored and bent about her sides where she was clasping him round the thighs.

Angela ran down the path, leaving the front gate open and opening the passenger door of the Mini. Flick hurried too. Her steps were as rapid but much shorter, her knees bending a little more with each one till Charles's shoes scuffed the ground. She turned herself round at the car door, and he didn't have far to drop. Flick sat on the pavement while Angela reached round her to secure the man's perch on the car seat.

'You've got him looking very nice,' Maggie said.

Flick's face was flushed. The discs of fat in her cheeks verged on purple. Sweat plastered strands of hair across her skin.

'He never tied his own tie so well.'

The tie was crimson with a pattern of dark spots, like some microscopic view of a bloodstream. The knot was tiny and would have choked him were he still alive.

'What are you going to do now?' Maggie asked.

Flick was breathless, so Angela spoke for her.

'We'll swing his legs inside the car, then hold him in place with the seatbelt.'

'That's good. I'll leave you to it. I see you've got it all thought out. Don't rush, though. You need a rest, Flick. Perhaps Miss Dirkin could make you a cup of tea? I'll wander back to the house and sort things out that end. I'll see you back there when you're ready.'

Maggie hadn't planned on going back to the house, but planning was not always necessary for a journey. Motion was.

'You can't leave me,' Flick panted. 'Not with him. Not on my own.'

Maggie studied the girl.

'We are all on our own,' she said. 'Ultimately. We each have to practise.'

The dark wet patch around her grandmother's backside was at Flick's eye-level as the skirt swished about the lady's legs, and Maggie walked away.

CHAPTER 3

B eech trees partnered each other on either side of the drive, which was so long it narrowed to a point before turning to run up to Mawsby Hall. Acres of grass spread back beyond the trees, opening up a world much broader than Flick's usual one. Her hands usually relaxed on the steering wheel as she entered the grounds, and her body unlocked from its tension.

Not this time though.

The ribs of the steering wheel bit into her palms. She took the curve slowly, staring ahead but more anxious about any movement to her side. The corpse leaned against its seatbelt but stayed upright. Skiing glasses from her glove compartment were wedged across his face, in case his eyes snapped open. The reflection in the narrow band of darkness distorted the passing trees and sky.

Flick accelerated into third gear. The passing trees repeated themselves to give her the sense of going nowhere.

She wound down the window. There was no breeze.

There was no air.

The dead man beside her had swallowed it all.

Sod it.

She stamped down her foot and roared ahead, reaching one hand out to hold her grandfather in position as she turned a corner.

The house was ahead of her now. It bulked square and grey, with rows of blank windows. She considered crunching her wheels across the gravelled path at the front, but swerved instead up the slope that carried the driveway around the back of the house, then coasted down to the stable yard at the far side.

Her car stopped. Flick jumped out and slammed shut her door.

The tourist season had not yet begun. The tea-room and shop were closed. The yard was empty.

This close season normally suited Flick. It left her free to explore the house and grounds without being viewed as a curiosity. Today though she needed people. Even tourists would have done. Anyone that lived and breathed and could speak and walk.

The buildings in the yard were friendlier, of the same grey stone blocks as the house, but lower and topped with slate roofs that were furred with moss. She liked the clock tower that stood on the angle of the building, with its white wooden slats and peaked roof. An iron cockerel crowned it, spinning round in the direction of the wind, and though the clock had stopped that had always been so. Time was different at Mawsby Hall. Time-keeping was a hobby, not a pressure. When the clocks inside the house were wound they ran at their own speed and soon whirred and chimed at different times. The bells were amusing until they grew tiresome, when they were left to go silent once again.

Time didn't matter to the dead either.

Flick wanted something to happen.

Anything.

She needed proof that the morning was flowing forward in time and would carry her with it.

A crash came out from the second stable. Falling wood sounded against the stone floor and metal clattered upon it. Flick was moving towards it as her grandmother emerged, pushing a wheelchair.

'I knew we'd have one somewhere,' Maggie said, and bent to push the chair's arms further apart so the leather of the seat was stretched firm. 'They used the Hall as a convalescent home during the war, then left all their junk behind. More crutches than anything, but you never know what you'll find if you dig deep enough. I pulled this thing out from the back.'

'Is it for Grandpa?'

'He needs it more than we do, don't you think? How's he getting along in there?'

'It was horrible, Granny.'

Maggie could never really believe in her granddaughter's voice. It was too at odds with the girl's appearance. The voice was small, the girl was huge. The voice was antique, while her denim dungarees, T-shirt of yellow and white hoops, and trainers with pink flashes, were modern enough. The voice belonged to a Felicity, while the girl had chosen to be called Flick.

A shock would have to change or silence her some day. The voice as it was would never cope with an interesting life.

There was some tremor in it even now.

'You've never done it. You've never had to travel with a dead man. How do you think you'd like that, Granny? How do you think you'd get on?'

Maggie didn't have an answer, so she left the wheelchair and approached the girl instead.

It wasn't easy. Opening your arms and having someone small run into them, that was easy, but there was too much of this girl to accommodate. It was years since Flick had fitted into a pair of arms.

Maggie stroked the hair back from the girl's forehead, then rested her hand on Flick's shoulder. She managed a half-encircling hug.

It was a little like hugging a tree, but she held on till the girl began to relax.

'I couldn't have done it,' Maggie finally declared. 'I wouldn't even have gone to that house without you. I'd never have brought your grandfather back. It was a big thing I asked you to do. A huge thing. And you've done it.'

Maggie squeezed her hold a little tighter before letting go, then moved round the car to look in through the window at her husband.

'Could you help me just one more time?' Maggie opened the car door. 'If we turn him round so that his legs are outside I'll probably be able to help cradle him into the air. Then we'll drop him into the wheelchair and he can rest awhile.'

Maggie looked up to check that Flick was responding, then reached across her husband's lap to fumble with the catch for the seatbelt. She rattled and tugged at it till she felt Flick's hand on her shoulder.

It was a firm hand, that eased her back without gripping.
'Let me do it,' Flick said.

Maggie stepped back to give the girl room and Flick spun Charles round. His head drooped as he waited for his next move.

Maggie fetched the wheelchair and pulled on its brakes.

'That's fine,' Flick instructed. 'Hold it steady.'

Maggie obeyed, for the dead man was already tipped into the girl's hands and being carried toward her. The chair rocked back and pushed against her as he hit it, but she managed to hold it upright.

'Well done,' Maggie offered. 'I wish I had your strength.'

It took more than strength, though. Maggie decided to speak the thought while she had it.

'You've got a lot about you, Flick. That took a lot of doing.'

Flick had put her hands on her waist, preparing to pull herself up straight. First she showed a slight smile to her grandmother as she recognised what was being said.

'You rest over there a moment.' Maggie nodded toward a bench by the stable wall, then moved round to place Charles's hands over the armrests. They seemed stiffer already. The legs appeared to be locked into their crooked position. 'I'll take Chumpers for one more look over his land before we settle him indoors.'

She moved his legs forward a fraction to make sure he was leaning back, then pulled off the brakes and pushed him on toward the front of the house.

* * *

28

She didn't remove the glasses, pull his eyelids open or support his head. Charles was dead. It was pointless playing such games.

Somehow though it was right to have him slumped at the head of his estate.

Maggie looked across her newly inherited land. The estate truly belonged to her son Edward, while she had inherited a grace and favour status, but in effect it was all hers now. Nobody else wanted the place.

The view was soothing. A ha-ha edged their terrace, and beyond this sunken wall the land sloped down towards the wall that ran along the valley floor. The field lacked the sheep that were there when she first moved in, but there were still the individual trees to enjoy. At times she had sat beneath each one, the trunk at her back shielding her from the house, her view in front climbing from the wall and into a forest that mounted a hill.

And beyond that hill of trees was the sky.

She had never understood why the windows of the house didn't reflect that view of the sky. The windows were not blue but a dark, blank grey. The house was blind to everything around it.

It was silly to expect a dead man to be any different. Still, it would do no harm to speak her mind. He would not listen but she needed the practice.

'I warn you, Chumpers, I feel sick,' she began. 'I could throw up over your head any moment. You die in a slut's bed. I inherit the responsibility of Mawsby. That's no bargain, Chumpers. That's you having the last laugh.

'I accept of course. I have no choice. I have only one condition. You're deaf but it doesn't matter. You've never heard me. Hear me now, Chumpers. Hear me now.

'I shall not be buried as I am. I will live before I die. No village slut's bedroom for my end, Chumpers. I shall laugh. I shall learn to laugh until the last laugh is mine.'

Maggie paused to see what else she had to say. Nothing came.

In that case she would put an end to words. It was time for action.

She wheeled Charles around and pushed him back into the house's shadow.

* * *

Flick hadn't rested.

'I found two planks,' the girl said. 'They're just right. I've built a ramp. We can push Grandpa up from the conservatory straight into the house.'

What the girl called a conservatory was more like a miniature greenhouse, an extended porch that formed a side-entrance to the Hall. Maggie peered inside to inspect the girl's handiwork. She met the scent of geraniums that packed the shelves to either side, still waiting for the buds of their flowers.

'Perfect,' she agreed, and stepped back. 'You've propped the door open too. You won't need me.'

'Aren't you coming? Aren't you going to help?'

'I'll push him. Just so far.'

Maggie walked back to the chair, eased it over the front step, then rolled it forward till its wheels touched the ends of the two planks. The girl was sandwiched between the geraniums and the corpse. Maggie moved back so she could set herself free.

'Can you do the rest yourself? Wheel your grandfather through to the library. He'll be all right there. He loved the smell of the books.'

'Aren't you coming?'

'In a while perhaps. When I've taken some air.'

'Shouldn't I tell someone? Find Daddy? Call a doctor?'

'There's no rush. Chumpers has had enough attention. More won't improve things. Just leave his body to rest awhile. I'll see you out here when you've finished. We'll go for a walk.'

Flick waited a moment, but couldn't see that she had any choice. She gripped hold of the handles. The planks rose behind her as she crossed the threshold, then they clattered back to the ground.

'Well done, Chumpers,' she heard her grandmother say. 'You've ascended.'

CHAPTER 4

F LICK WALKED TO THE TERRACE when she could not find her grandmother outside. She spotted her some way down the slope of grass, folded into the shadows of an oak tree, her knees drawn up and her back against its trunk. Flick waved but the figure didn't look up. She left the terrace and walked down the slope towards her.

'I couldn't find you,' Flick complained. 'You said you'd wait in the yard.'

'You've found me.' Maggie smiled up at her. 'I sat this side of the tree so that you could. How's your grandfather?'

'I left him by the library window. You can probably see him.'

Flick turned to check if this was so.

She had walked further down the slope than she thought. Mawsby Hall was so reduced she could frame it between her thumb and forefinger. The library windows were narrow but tall, fronting the ground floor of the east wing. She could make out nothing behind them.

'You won't see anything through those windows,' her grandmother confirmed. 'It's a curious virtue of the place. We can look out, but others don't get to look in.'

Maggie stood up and started down the slope.

'Where are you going?'

'For our walk,' Maggie replied. 'Aren't you coming?'

The air had been washed clear by the night's storm, the sunlight was gentle, the sky was blue. It had the makings of a very pleasant day. Grass softened Maggie's steps and the slope sped her on.

Flick uprooted herself and ran to catch up.

Maggie paused by the wall and pulled at a string looped around her neck. They had reached a solid wooden gate. The key to it rose out of the front of Maggie's dress. She lifted the string over her head so as to use it.

She was excited. She knew what lay behind the gate yet it always surprised her.

She took hold of the gate's handle, and pulled.

'There!' she said, but the triumph in her voice sounded doubtful. The old run of surprises weren't working any more.

Flick looked above her grandmother's head and saw a parade of tree trunks. Maggie had soaked up all the impact and left none for the girl. It wasn't till Maggie turned that Flick noticed the burst of life in the woman, the fun at play in her eyes.

'I do love forest land,' Maggie tried out in a sing-song voice, whether to cheer the girl or herself she did not know.

Flick tried to smile back, but Maggie was already on her way. She had chosen a path that cut across at the level rather than heading straight up the hill.

'Some call this Bluebell Wood,' she explained. 'There's much more to a woodland than its bluebells, but I know what they mean. Bluebells are such wonderful plants. They live in shadow but their green shines a light of its own. When their flowers come they dust this floor sky blue. It's the universe turned upside down so we can look down on the heavens. That's what a wood is, Flick. Heaven on earth.'

Flick stayed quiet.

She wasn't a stranger to this wood, for she knew where she was being led. She was last here as a child. The path wound along, enclosed by trees that were themselves almost smothered by rhododendrons, then the whole lot gave way. There was a clearing. She remembered how some of the rhododendron struggled across it but didn't get far. They were like trees that had chosen to bow down.

That was the sense she had as a child, when she first saw the building in the centre – to bow down or run away. It was so vast, so strange, it demanded some show of respect.

The path should be opening into the light of its clearing any moment.

Instead the wood grew darker.

Maggie didn't hesitate. She stepped over roots and the tangled arms of rhododendron, and ducked beneath branches.

A row of thicker trees emerged, their trunks a russet red, exceptionally straight. Flick was just a few steps away when she recognised them. They were not trees at all but the columns of the building. The base of each rested on the back of an elephant, pressing the animals down on their haunches. Each elephant rested on a stone balustrade.

Flick stepped back a little way to take in the building as a whole.

The climate had smeared a patina of dark grey over the sandstone blocks, but they still flushed pink beneath the skin.

The building was topped with four roofs, receding in waves of red tiles to reach a pedestal at the top. A stone chalice sat at this highest point, with a fluted top that tapered to a point and then nothing.

Between the chalice and its lid Flick made out a twig, the stem of a young tree. Saplings had planted themselves in place of the missing tiles, and grasses grew among the patches of moss. Branches of the rhododendron had stretched through the stone railings to colonise the covered walkway.

'Flick!' Maggie called.

The girl worked her way along a path around the side of the mausoleum, following her grandmother's voice.

'Have you been inside before?'

Flick shook her head.

Instead of going up to the door, Maggie headed in the opposite direction. A small patch of ground was laid out with wooden crosses and stones, and surrounded by a fence. The fence was low. Maggie stepped over it.

'It's all changed,' Flick said. 'I don't remember any grass here last time. This was just a sandy area. And I don't remember any trees. Now they're even growing out of the roof, and these rhodies are everywhere.'

'The rhodies were a novelty once. One of your ancestors had them shipped over from the Himalayas. Now they flourish like weeds.'

'Doesn't anybody look after the place? It's just a jungle.'

'It's wild. There's no harm in a little wilderness. The pets' cemetery has filled up a bit since you were last here too. This is Lizzie. Do you remember her? My cavalier spaniel.'

Maggie bent down, pulled out the wooden cross that marked the grave, and reached inside the hole. Flick waited for Lizzie to be dragged out by the ears, the soil shaken off her fur and the creature reintroduced.

Instead Maggie pulled out a key. It was ten inches long, of blackened brass.

'I keep it hidden here,' she explained. 'It's too heavy to carry backwards and forwards.'

Maggie stepped over the fence and up the steps to the door of the mausoleum.

The door was of darkened oak, banded with cast iron, locked into its frame and behind a step so that no light filtered inside. It was the kind of door Flick would expect of a castle, some Transylvanian castle door that creaked open to receive visitors. That it didn't creak, simply wheezed, was no comfort.

Maggie pushed it open and slipped inside.

'Come on,' she called back.

Her voice chased itself around the interior to gather resonance before Flick heard it.

'Don't be afraid.'

Flick took the key from the door and slid it into the pocket of her dungarees before stepping inside. With one hand still on the handle she peered around, finally spotting the shape of her grandmother on the other side of the door, just a few feet away.

'Well close it then,' Maggie said.

'But it's so dark.'

'Close it!'

The tone annoyed Flick, and made her act too fast. She slammed the door shut before she could jump back outside. She was closed in.

In a mausoleum.

In its pitch black.

'I want to show you something,' Maggie said.

There was a noise, the sound of metal turning. It seemed to be moving up the wall above them both, though in the dark where all sounds chased around to clash against their echo it was hard to tell.

Maggie laughed, a breathy laugh, amused at the effort she was putting into this new game.

Flick found she could see her, a dim figure at first till the lines grew sharper and Maggie was revealed in the glimmering of light. With one hand she was holding a metal pole that spindled up toward the ceiling, while with the other she turned a cranking handle. The pole rattled in its brackets and far above them cogs turned and flaps dropped to let in daylight. A layer of the roof was made of wooden panels. As Maggie turned the handle, they opened like petals of a flower toward the sky.

'I love doing that.' Maggie let go of the handle and stepped into the middle of the space to look up. 'I feel like God turning on a new day.'

'What happens if you do it at night?'

'I switch on the stars.'

'And if it's cloudy?'

'I only said I *feel* like God. Don't be so earnest, Flick. I'm not God. I don't know how to open up the clouds. This was just a game. I'm only me. And these are your great-great-etcetera-uncles. That's how we end up when we finish playing our games.'

They were obviously coffins, laid on a shelf that surrounded the room, but they were made of stone instead of wood. Names and dates were engraved on the ends that faced Flick, but that was their only ornamentation. It was all so bare inside these walls, so bare and cold. Flick welcomed the light but still felt frozen. She had come far enough on this day's journey. She wanted to curl up against herself and wait to grow warm.

'Six brothers went to India. Five died and one survived to bring the others home. That one there.'

Maggie pointed to a coffin that looked exactly like the others.

'Now they're all embalmed together.'

'What did they die of?'

'Illness. Plague. Disease. What does it matter? The survivor died of old age but it all amounts to the same thing. Except maybe he wouldn't look so beautiful if we opened him up. It was he who had this place built. The stone was chiselled out of India, carved in workshops just outside Calcutta, then shipped over here along with the workforce to erect it. There's a handsome picture of the operation in the dining hall, lots of little brown men scurrying over the near-completed pile while your uncle stands in a frock coat and looks on. Those are two of the workers, there and there.'

Two small coffins, a good foot shorter than the others, edged the row of five like bookends.

'They're from one of the ex-colonies. Indian workers. They died during the construction, so your uncle had them built in.'

'They must be cold,' Flick noted. 'They should have been taken home. This place gives me the shivers.'

Though that wasn't true. To shiver you have to thaw a little first.

'Your grandfather felt funny about this place. He seldom came near it. Said it was poisoned. Saw it as a symbol of the whole estate. Stolen from India and left here to rot.'

'How could the whole estate have come from India?'

'Your great-great-etcetera-grandfather, these men's father, was a solicitor in London. Worthy but dull. Six sons left him for India, one came back to join the landed gentry. Mawsby was built on the profits from trade, a trade in the natural produce of India. That was your grandfather's argument. He saw everything as coming from India, just like these sandstone blocks.'

Maggie reached out to touch the fabric of the building.

'Who are all the others?' Flick had started to look around. 'The shelves are full.'

'Nearly.'

Maggie walked toward a wide slot that was empty of coffins but displayed half a dozen urns.

'They spoke of adding an extra shelf when Chumpers was a boy, he told me. Then they switched to cremation. I'm pleased. It's more fun to end up in an urn. Like a championship trophy for a life well lived. This is your family, Flick. This is Chumpers's mother, this his father. Gathered to await you. Your progenitors.'

Maggie rounded the last word out, as though its syllables might combine into a joke, and moved a hand toward the shelf. She picked up a child's slate in a simple wooden frame. There was writing on it.

'It's from Chumpers,' she announced, then read it to herself. 'A farewell note.'

Curiosity prompted Flick to move at last. She left the door and crossed the floor, looking up briefly to where the roof stretched into shadow above her.

The message was written in blue chalk, spelled out in evenly spaced block capitals.

HELLO MAGGIE.
WELL DONE.
YOU'VE SURVIVED ME.
TIME FOR A LITTLE ADVENTURE OF YOUR OWN.
DON'T LEAVE ME ON THE SHELF.
TAKE ME HOME.

'He didn't sign it,' Flick commented. 'He didn't send his love.'

'That's his style.'

Maggie took the slate back. She pulled up the pleats of her skirt and rubbed the message away, its dust gathering as a cloud on the dark blue silk.

'It doesn't mean much,' Flick said. 'We've already brought him home.'

'That isn't what he meant.'

'So where is home?'

'Home is where you first find peace.' Maggie set the slate back down on the shelf of urns. 'For Chumpers it's somewhere far away.'

Up above them they heard the sharp flutter of wings. They looked up as a bird curved a line of flight down to land on the end of one of the coffins, a more recent one veneered in black marble.

'It's a starling,' Maggie said.

She had started to admire starlings of late. There was something mocking about the way they filled the branches of a winter tree, packing it with their shapes of blackened leaves, then rose in a chittering cloud to leave the tree bare. They hopped across the death of winter, took it as their playground, scavenged for its pickings.

The bird flew across the chamber of the mausoleum, so close to their faces they felt the wind of its wings, and settled on one of the uncles of that first Indian adventure.

'It's trapped.'

Flick flapped her hands by her sides as though giving the bird a suggestion of what to do, and moved backwards as she watched it.

'It's stuck. It can't get out.'

'It got in. Of course it can get out. There's the strip of daylight up above us. The bird must sense that as well as we can.'

The creature didn't seem desperate to Maggie. With the onset of spring it was just taking its chance to revisit death for a while. It would explore a little, then fly on its way.

Flick's shout was muffled by fear into a squeak of breath as the bird skittered past her. She wrapped her arms about her head. When she looked up the bird had settled on one of the urns.

'The poor thing's lost,' she said, and ran with the words toward the door, clearing the space in four strides and hauling at the latch to swing the door wide.

The sudden move, the rush of light and air, startled the bird. Maggie watched it rise, a spiral of flight that took it up toward the ceiling and out through one of the flaps.

Flick stood to one side to let the bird through. She paused a moment to realise it had left by a different route, then made her own escape.

Maggie took her time. She wound the handle to seal the flaps. The chamber passed into dusk, but she didn't feel like God any more. Just Maggie with her own life to face.

She backed into the light from the doorway, then pulled the door closed in front of her.

* * *

'I love it here,' Maggie declared.

Flick had lowered her body onto the rock a little way below, so that despite her climb she was yet to see the view. Maggie was taking it all in.

The forest hadn't given way. It continued down the hill, but this rock they were on was so large no tree could get a purchase. Behind her, in the direction Flick was facing, Maggie could have seen Mawsby Hall pretty much at the same level as herself. She chose instead her favourite perch on a rounded piece of the rock. The stone was bald and warmed a little by the sun. She let her legs drop in front of her and looked out beyond the trees to a plain of fields and the town.

'I came and sat here when I was first married,' she said. 'I played a game in my head. This hill was a petrified tidal wave. This rock was its crest. Some day when I was up here the force would melt. I'd ride the wave till it swept across all of this little land of England and dropped me somewhere new.'

She closed her eyes to imagine the scene, as she had done many times before, but could only sense the sun upon her eyelids and hear Flick pull herself up to settle on the rock beside her.

'Rocks don't melt, Flick. Sticks don't swim. And ladies of a certain age are prone to crumple and die if they don't move about a little. Ache though we do, we have to kick out for ourselves. I'm going away. I'm going to walk down this hill and keep on going.'

'I don't think so, Granny. You're in shock. You're strange by nature. Grandpa's death will make you stranger. It doesn't mean you have to take up exercise.'

'I'm not talking exercise. Exercise is for the horses. Exercise is for the prison yard. It's what one does when stuck in a life that simply goes round and round. I'm freed from such a life now, Flick. I'm going to go straight for a while. Keep on going and see where it takes me.'

'You can't.'

'Can't?' Maggie looked at the girl. 'Children set limits. Even husbands set limits. But spare me the limits set by grandchildren.'

'But what about Grandpa?'

'What about him?'

'He's dead.'

'Exactly.'

'There are things to do. Doctors to call. Arrangements to be made.'

'Call your father. Such things are his forte.'

'And what am I meant to tell Dad? That you've run away?'

'If you like.'

'Listen to me, Gran.'

Maggie turned to face her granddaughter. She would show a little patience. There was something endearing about the earnestness of the young.

'I can stay with you. Help you through it. Just a few days and the worst will be over. You can have a holiday then. For now though we need you here. People can't just run when their husbands die.'

'Why not?'

'It isn't done.'

'Oh really, Flick!' Maggie turned away to look at the landscape beyond. 'You're so young, yet so stuck. "It isn't done" indeed! If something isn't done, that's exactly the reason to go out and do it. What do you want out of life? A little bit of fun, or marks for good behaviour?'

'Is good behaviour so bad?'

'It's so dull. Society sets the rules, Flick. That doesn't mean it's wise. Society is nothing but a set of old habits.'

'We won't invite society. It can be a small family funeral.'

'I'll pray for you all from afar.'

'Did you hate Grandpa so much?'

'Hate?' Maggie faced Flick again. 'I hate cold cuts of lamb in aspic. I hate brown water gushing through the taps in the bath. I hate cheap wine and Spanish champagne. But I never hate people. Those I don't like I simply pity.'

'Did you like Grandpa so little?'

'You know, child...' Maggie paused to give it some thought, making sure she wasn't being unfair. 'I suppose I did. There really wasn't very much to like. We had a contract. Till death us do part. I've seen it through. Does that sound callous?'

Flick nodded her head.

'Perhaps I'm not likeable either,' Maggie mused. 'I haven't been myself for so many years, I don't know any more. We'll see.'

'I like you,' Flick admitted. 'I love you. I just wish you were more responsible at times.'

'You asked where your grandfather's home was...' Maggie paused and Flick waited for more. 'It's in the jungles of Thailand. Beside the River Kwai. It was a place of horror. He held friends in his arms as they died. Their spirits hung around to hold him in turn. That is as much as he knew about peace. He asks me to take him home. That is my last responsibility. To return him to his friends by the River Kwai.'

'So you'll wait for his ashes?'

'That's too much to ask.' Maggie considered the options. 'Post him to me, my dear.'

'Post him?'

'It shouldn't cost much once he's ashes. Go along with all that's asked. Let them place him in their mausoleum. Then empty his urn into a plastic bag.'

'You want me to post his ashes to Thailand?'

'Not there. Post him to Bangladesh. Care of World Vision. You'll find their address in my bureau. I'm going to see our little boy.' Maggie noticed Flick's confusion. 'I'm sorry, my dear. You're so methodical, you're forcing me to plan ahead all in a rush. Do you know about Amar? We've been sponsoring him for some years. Family guilt has been trickling a little money back to East India. They send us photos and school reports now and again, but really Amar has never been anything but a standing order. It will be fun to see the boy for real.'

'Bangladesh isn't fun, Granny. It's poor. We studied it at school.'

'Good. If there's no fun in Bangladesh, I'll have to find it in myself. That's where it's been missing.'

Maggie looked at her granddaughter, then picked up her right hand to pat it.

'Go back to the house, dear Flick. Call your father. He'll be along soon. Leave things in his hands. He's a capable man.'

'What shall I tell him?'

'Oh, there's plenty of things to talk about. Your grandfather's just died. In the bed of another woman. Death and betrayal. It's enough to throw any wife a little off-balance. Tell him I needed to go away and think things through. Tell him I say Miss Dirkin is welcome at the funeral, and that I shall conduct my own ceremony of remembrance. Focus on your grandfather's adultery. They'll understand why a wife might find the place and manner of his death quite unacceptable. That's something everyone will understand. Give your father my love, and tell him I'll be in touch. I'm going to walk away now. Allow me a couple of hours to get clear before they send the posse after me.'

'You can't just go. Where's your luggage?'

Maggie tapped her bag. It was an evening bag stitched out of black, with shiny beads and a silver metal clasp. The addition of a thin leather strap hooked it over her shoulder to leave her hands free.

'But it's tiny.'

'This is the credit card age. It's good I've lived so long. Travelling lightly has never been easier. Goodbye, Flick.'

Maggie pressed her lips against Flick's cheek. The cheek was moist, her lips were dry.

'Will you write?' Flick asked.

'Postcards.' This was a commitment. Maggie saw how swiftly her freedom was cramping itself, but the girl was in need.

'I'll send you postcards,' she promised, then turned to drop her foot down the rock face and find herself a perch.

'You can't climb, Granny,' Flick said. 'Not in those shoes.'

Maggie smiled at her. The shoes were flat soled and black, made of kid leather that fit Maggie's feet with the closeness of gloves. They were old but then her feet were old. Feet and shoes had aged together. As Maggie trod down the rocks, it seemed the goat leather had returned to its element. Her balance was perfect. Her legs were in control. Flick watched the smile disappear, then the glowing eyes, before the white cloud of her grandmother's hair also dropped beyond this near horizon.

Postcards ...

London
Been to the Embassy. Visa's ready in two days. Shall holiday till then. Swanning up the Thames on a boat like a Queen. Wave at everyone and some wave back. Passed Tower of London. Walls like Mawsby Hall. Shuddered then laughed, and stayed on board. Feeling free. River suits my mood. Bought a day pass so shall go up and down. Sunlight falls on the city. It's textured with history, but then aren't we all?
Love,
Maggie

The writing was tiny. Flick squinted to read it, then turned the card over to look at its picture. It showed Trafalgar Square. The fountains were coloured in light blue and the circling buses a bright red. Nelson was standing on top of his column in the middle. He had lost an arm and an eye, but still he looked downhill toward the Thames: the Englishman on his island who dreamed of floating away.

There were two more postcards.

One in black and white showed a little girl in a party frock tugging at the tunic of a guardsman, who was standing impassive in front of his sentry box.

The other was a sunset study of the sea, strips of darkness and orange with the silhouettes of seabirds flecking the skyline.

The handwriting was larger, and the message spread over both cards.

Brighton
Put money in box to help restore west pier. It tugs at the shore like a graceful old liner. Trying to rip Brighton away from England and out to sea. A good idea. Computer tunes and girls in wet T-shirts on the east pier. Stood with sea below me. Didn't have fortune told. Shall make it up as I go along. Naked men on beach. Skulking in hollows among pebbles. Trench warfare, shooting glances at each other. Didn't see me though. I'm invisible. Took off shoes and walked into sea. So cold, so moving, moving all the time. Broke bread from sandwich and threw it into sky. Seagull caught it. Refuelled in flight. What flight, Flick. I see it now. Seagulls don't cry. They laugh. I see how seagulls belong.
Love,
Maggie

The last postcard was of an airliner flying into the blue. Maggie headed the message *Gatwick Airport 18th March*, then switched to block capitals.

KEEP THE HOME FIRES BURNING.
LOVE,
MAGGIE

CHAPTER 5

THE MAN IN THE SEAT NEXT TO MAGGIE had a long beard but clean-shaven jowls. His hair was dark grey. He introduced himself as a District Commissioner for the Boy Scouts called Roy Metcalf, and helped buckle her seatbelt. The pressure of take-off pressed her back against her seat and tilted her skywards.

The trolley came. Roy ordered himself a whisky. Maggie ordered champagne and was given a quarter bottle. Taittinger. Acceptable for a start. She sipped and watched the tiny plane on the video screen nudge its course across the Channel. Below her the view was obscured by clouds. And perhaps a little smoke.

'My husband's being cremated today, I think.' She turned to her neighbour. 'Perhaps right now, as we drink. Are you married, Roy?'

He blinked before answering.

'I was.'

Maggie's open gaze forced him to say more. He turned his head away as he spoke.

'We separated. Then she died.'

'You were married. That doesn't go away. Was she cremated?'

Roy nodded, then leaned out into the aisle to look for the return of the drinks trolley.

'Did they give you the remains?'

'She had remarried.'

'But you went to the funeral?'

Roy nodded again.

'I don't care for cremations. Maybe it's my husband's jungle stories from the war. He told of bodies flung on open fires. Cholera victims largely. As they lay on the flames their muscles contracted. The corpses seemed to jerk back to life. Are you going far?'

'To Oman.' Maggie watched the skin of Roy's throat contract as he gulped the whisky down. 'To visit my daughter.'

'She lives there?'

'Her husband's an engineer. They have two children.'

'I have a grandchild.'

Maggie fetched a photograph out of her tiny bag. It showed Flick and Edward, Maggie's son, standing to either side of herself. Maggie was the only one smiling.

'My husband wasn't so tall,' she said. 'I don't know how we spawned such monsters.'

Maggie stared into the photo, then drifted into a doze. She was woken to receive a tray of food, and claimed another glass of champagne. It was poured from a full-size bottle this time. Laurent Perrier. Pink. Maggie reached her finger up to the bottle's neck as it was being withdrawn. The steward smiled and set it down on her table.

The in-flight movie was silly. She turned the channel back to the screen that showed the aircraft's progress. The little plane nudged forward, from one continent already too big to call her own and into another. A full moon shone outside. She moved her head so as to maintain the image of the moon in the centre of her round window.

'Are you alone now, Roy?' she suddenly asked. 'Or have you got a mistress?'

She watched the man's profile blotch red.

'I'm sorry,' she said. 'That's not one of the questions we ask, is it? I used to know. I used to be sure of such things. My social gaffes were always intentional. It's strange how some skills vanish. My husband had a mistress. She's very likely crying at her loss as we fly. I thought of her, then wondered about you.'

He turned his head just slightly toward her, smiled with the side of his mouth she could see, and fixed his headset over his ears.

* * *

'You're old enough,' she remarked to Roy later. 'You must remember the war.'

He turned to her. His eyes were open but sleep lay just behind them. It was up to her to carry the conversation.

'My home was a house in the countryside. The war raged elsewhere and sirens wailed from a distant town and over our fields. Looking through the window just now, it's made me think. I helped hang blackout curtains. Sometimes I draped the material over my head and simply sat there, knowing the rest of the world had disappeared. My experience was small and I wished it to be bigger. Now I'm up in the sky. There are whole cities down there. I can see them. I know them by their lights. But if they turned their lights off, they'd cease to exist.'

Her video screen kept flashing between alternate maps. The familiar one showed Arabia on the right-hand side. In the other it had shifted to the left. Europe had been displaced by India and beyond.

A single light flared in the space outside. Large and unsteady, it was the flame from an oil platform out at sea. The pilot's voice came over the speakers in the ceiling. Such a steady and sophisticated voice, Maggie knew herself to be in good hands on first hearing it. Now he announced they would soon be landing. She felt a pang of regret.

She followed instructions, righting the back of her seat and fastening her belt. The lights of Dubai began to appear in a neat white grid, narrow at first then broadening into a city. The engines changed pitch. They swallowed their familiar noise and roared back still louder, a roar that shook the body of the plane.

Maggie reached out for help. It lay nearby in the form of Roy's hand. She clutched at it with both hands, curling its fingers round to hold her own.

Roy's was a plump hand but the skin was dry. The texture surprised her. She looked down at the hairs that curled across its back, and clustered in whorls on the knuckles. Red patches flaked the white of the skin. The fingers were pudgy. As she loosened her grip she felt the callused stubs where the nails had been bitten back.

'It's perfectly all right,' her neighbour assured her. 'The noise is quite normal. It always changes like that on landing.'

54

She smiled, but had no interest in what he was saying. The plane could do what it liked. She wanted her hands returned to her. The man's hand tried to close around hers but she pulled them back then settled them on her lap.

'You're right,' she said. 'Silly me.'

A line of palm trees grew larger along the fringe of the airport.

This was a new world.

She needed no old man's hand to guide her through it.

Her body shivered inside the fresh roar of the plane. The touchdown was surprisingly gentle.

Postcard

Maggie found a postcard in Dubai Airport. It showed a train of camels walking the ridge of a sand dune. She waited until the next segment of her flight to write it.

Karachi
Switched flights at Dubai. Left luxury behind. Pakistan sweating beyond the portholes. Militant stewardesses won't let me stand up, let alone leave. We're quarantined in this nasty, narrow plane. They're spraying huge cans of insecticide across the ceiling as I write. Next stop, Dhaka. Where I shall sleep, and sleep.
love
Maggie

PART TWO

Foreign Fields

CHAPTER 6

MAGGIE WOKE TO THE BLACKNESS of closed shutters. Her bed had turned hard. She slid her hand along the sheet and curled her fingers around the edge of the mattress. It was half an inch thick. Beneath it her fingernails scraped a sheet of hardboard.

She kept her hand moving up to the side of her face, where the fingers caught on an elastic string and pushed it high. The darkness lifted and she held up the black nylon pads that had covered her eyes. It was an eye-mask, part of an airline's courtesy pack of toiletries.

She ignored a slight knocking on her door. Her senses were busy coming round to the moment, but they hadn't got there yet.

If she was in her own four-poster, the drapes had changed. They used to be of thick white damask with silver leaves threaded down the folds. The material here was rotted away, leaving nothing but its net behind.

The door was rapped again, by the knuckle of a finger.

Maggie pulled herself up the bed till she was sitting. She looked through the gauze and about her room.

Her bed was narrow. The net curtains, to all four sides and above, were a dirty grey and splattered. A stray leg was cocked out of the black flattened body stuck in the nearest brown spot. That spot was her own blood.

Maggie raised the palms of her hands to examine them for stains. Her memory was coming back now. She had danced around this bed the previous night, clapping folds of the curtain between her hands, aiming for the mosquitoes that lived there.

This was one she caught.

Maggie stretched forward to feel around her ankles, rubbing her fingers over the little pustules of bites, scratching her nails loosely over the surface.

The room was gloomy. The mustard yellow paint on the walls was pocked with further splotches of blood and insects. Maggie looked across the concrete floor to her suitcase sitting on a wooden stool. The room's only other furniture was a plain wooden table and chair.

A yellow nylon curtain hung on a wire across the window. Its bottom stopped just short of the sill. A pair of eyes, large and brown, looked back at Maggie through the gap.

'Miss Maggie?'

There were railings at the window, but no glass. A finger stuck through beside the face and lifted the curtain high.

'Miss Maggie?'

She blinked back and the face smiled.

'You are awake, yes? May I come in?'

He paused for a moment, then lowered the curtain. A moment later the door opened and he stepped in. Maggie did not require deference from her servants. Those who took pride in their function ghosted around the periphery of her life, for that was the natural thing for them to do. They might lever open a window, push back the shutters, bring or remove her breakfast tray, perhaps pass a comment on the weather, but they would never impose their personality. This youth entered the room as though it were his own. Rubber sandals thwacked the soles of his bare brown feet. Black nylon trousers had been worn to a sheen on his thighs. He wore his tangerine shirt loose, its sleeves rolled above the elbows. His body was slight, yet he carried it with disturbing confidence. He was some lithe young animal, and her room was his habitat.

'You should lock this,' he said, and pushed the bolt home to show her how. 'We have security. A twenty-four hour security man. But sometimes he sleeps. And you are a woman alone. You sleep well, Miss Maggie?'

Maggie collected herself. The cup of tea he was carrying made her realise she was thirsty. Her needs and the true state of her situation came back to her.

This is Sepen, she reminded herself. Slight in build but not a child. Perhaps a man.

What good was his smiling like that when she wished to be angry?

'There is no air,' she complained. 'You promised me air-conditioning.'

'Fan-cooled, Miss Maggie.'

He turned a dial on the wall. A large propeller whirred up a breeze from the ceiling then churned it into a gale. The shaft was not straight but wobbled as though working its way loose.

'Turn it down.'

'It will not. It is broken. Only one speed. Deluxe.'

'Then turn it off.'

He moved the dial. The propeller eased back into still blades.

'I bring you tea.'

He set the cup and saucer down on the table then walked round her bed, piling the walls of net curtain up onto the canopy. She was revealed, sitting there in her long white cotton nightdress.

'The English like tea, yes? All the time.'

The cup was chipped, but she sipped at it.

'This is sugared,' she said.

Sepen smiled.

'I don't take sugar.'

She drank another mouthful though. The sugar smoothed the liquid down her throat.

'You said there was a view.'

'There is a window.'

'But it's internal. It looks out onto the corridor. A corridor isn't a view. And you said the hotel was clean.'

'It is clean.'

'It is filthy. And the private bathroom?'

'It is bad?'

Sepen walked through the bathroom door and turned on each of the faucets. She heard the water splash down.

'It is fine. Everything working.'

'There is no toilet.'

'It is here.'

'It is a hole in the ground. The shower is a pipe with its end cut off. The water is cold. Am I to stand on the concrete and be hosed down like a dog?'

He came out of the bathroom. She had finished her tea so handed the cup and saucer to him.

'Why did I believe you at the airport? There were many others. Why did I trust myself to you? Was it technique?'

She watched him slide his finger down the bridge of his nose. It was a gesture to show he was thinking, but it was also part of the answer. The nose was so straight, so perfect, so beautiful. She had followed his nose.

'I am good, Miss Maggie. I understand. You come to the airport. The noise, the shouting, the hands on your bag. When your eyes see me they can rest. I stand on the outside. I hand you my card. I say "Can I help you, Madame?" '

The business card was presented beneath his hand. The fingers were slender. The gesture was delicate. Maggie longed for delicate things. She was the type to follow a butterfly through a wilderness.

'I speak your language. I say what you want to hear.'

'You tell me your lies.'

'I tell you my truths. You hear lies. That is not my fault. Everything in Bangladesh is different.' He looked about the room from where he stood. 'This is a good room. A quiet room. You will like this hotel, Miss Maggie. It is friendly. It is away from the street and the noise. It is cheap. There are big hotels. Luxury hotels. Why do you come to Bangladesh, and go to those? You are not that type of woman.'

'I am,' Maggie remembered. 'That is exactly the type I am.'

'That woman does not walk through airport doors on her own. The hotel sends her a chauffeur.'

63

'Telephone them now. They can send one here.'

'You are searching. You have come to see the little boy you sponsor. You tell me this. You are looking for your life, and you will find it in people. That is the way. I will help you.'

'I can choose my own people.'

'You chose me. You say that is a bad choice. So you are not good at choosing. You need my help.'

He tipped back his head to catch a laugh. Maggie saw the white row of his teeth, the strands of dark hair fall behind his ears, his throat tauten and his chest rise against his tangerine shirt. It was a high unaffected laugh of a child. The tea-cup rattled on its saucer to join in.

'I need no one,' Maggie said.

He was still enjoying his joke as he walked toward the door.

'I will leave you now. You can get dressed. You will have breakfast downstairs. Then we will phone your organisation. They will send a car to take us to your boy.' He pulled back the bolt and opened the door. 'If you need me, call. Call Sepen.'

She needed one thing.

To be left alone.

That was all.

He closed the door. The wind of it stirred some dust in that corner of the room. A shape darted out, large and black. A mouse she thought. It dashed across the open floor, stopped, and switched track. She saw the gloss of its round, armoured body, and heard the clicking of its feet as it sped toward the shadows beneath her bed.

It was a cockroach.

'Sepen!' she yelled.

* * *

Maggie remembered winding her watch forward to effect the time difference as her plane dropped into Dhaka airport. It should be correct, yet it told her the time was two o'clock. She walked down to the small reception hall where Sepen was waiting.

'What is the time?' she asked him.

He bent his head round to look at her watch.

'Two o'clock,' he said.

'I can read my own watch. I asked you what the proper time was.'

'Two o'clock. In the afternoon. And you will have your breakfast?'

He pointed the way to the dining room.

'It can't be afternoon.'

'You travelled a long way. You are tired. You slept well. Now you will have breakfast.'

'Don't be silly. I can't have breakfast in the afternoon. I have to adjust. What do you eat at this time of day?'

'I don't eat.'

'You must.'

'It is Ramadan. We do not eat or drink till the sun goes down. The kitchen is closed. But the boy is making you tea and toast. I will phone your organisation.'

'It's too late. Perhaps I can go tomorrow.'

'They can send a car now. You will have time. This afternoon I have an appointment at the airport. Tomorrow I can be with you. I will show you Dhaka. You are a woman. It is not good for you to go alone.'

He lifted the receiver.

'You have the number?' he asked.

'Do you speak English?'

She used the tone practised on French teenagers who sometimes drove up in coaches and ran amok in the gift shop at Mawsby Hall. They strutted about, thrusting their youth in people's faces and stuffing their pockets with souvenirs, until they heard her voice. She shepherded them with her tongue until they stood in an orderly line and held out their goods to be paid for. Youth was like a virus she had to keep in check.

She had two beings inside her; the schoolmistress and the girl.

The phone in Sepen's hand buzzed in the silence.

'Put the phone down, Sepen. And listen. I am NOT going to visit the boy today. Do you understand me? Is that simple enough? It is too late. Perhaps tomorrow. Perhaps not. I will decide. I don't need you now, Sepen. You have an appointment at the airport. So please go.'

He set the heavy black receiver on its cradle and stepped up to her.

'Miss Maggie. You are tired. Do not be angry. Do not be angry with Sepen. I try to help. Only help. Come, I smell toast. Toast and tea. You can eat, and then you can rest.'

'I don't need rest. I need some air.'

'There is a park. Very near. A park like in England. You can go there. But first, come and eat.'

He took her hand. His hold was gentle but he squeezed lightly, as though pulsing some of his energy into her. His hand was cool, the skin was smooth. She was too tired to play schoolmistress any longer.

The toast smelled good.

Maggie let the girl in her be led away.

CHAPTER 7

FINE CALVES WERE GOOD IN A MAN. Maggie watched the veins bulge in the tensed calves of the rickshaw-driver. They were not bad. The long beard tapering to a point, on the other hand, was a turn-off. It drew the sweat from his face. He pleaded for her to climb into his empty carriage.

'No!' she repeated, tired of politeness. He had been shadowing her for five minutes. 'No No No NO!'

The road was crazy with rickshaws. She jumped to avoid one, stalled to miss another, then spurted for the far pavement as other rickshaws with vacant seats tried to scoop her in their direction. She hurried through a gate and into the park.

The grass was thick and dark green.

One man pushed the handles of an antique lawnmower while another pulled at a rope attached to it. The blades grated round and coughed above the ground. Two hens pecked through the newly mown lawn. Strings looped around their necks led back to a man's hands. He crouched on the grass, his white cotton uniform of trousers and top smart enough but with hair that could have been cut with a stone and eyes that stared unblinking. His hens picked up the focus of his madness. All three creatures turned their heads and and watched Maggie pass.

She headed for a line of trees and the shade they spilled over the path and lawns. The ground dipped into a pool behind them, its water a grey tinged with the red of its mud.

Women stood by the shallows at its edges, bright colours of pinks and blues and greens stretched across their laundry laid out on the grass to dry.

And small children darted about; some boys in baggy shorts and a couple of girls in straight dresses streaked with mud, the others just in glossy skins. They splashed and dived, jumped and shouted and laughed.

And they saw her.

'Taka,' one boy shouted, naming the local currency.

The others took it up.

'Taka taka taka.'

It wasn't a chorus. They each shouted for themselves, using their hands to mime how she should throw them coins to dive for.

'Taka taka taka.'

Maggie wore a blouse, and an Indian-print skirt she bought in Brighton from the same shop as her flip-flops. It had no pockets to turn inside-out, to show she had no money with her.

She waved. 'Bye-bye.'

The first boy was out of the water and slithering up the slope as she turned. The others splashed their way to follow as she hurried along the path.

'Taka.'

A hand placed itself inside her own, so tiny it didn't cover her palm but the fingers tickled forward till they caught hold.

'Taka.'

'No taka,' Maggie said as hands clasped hers, and other hands gripped her lower arms. She walked on as children skipped beside her. 'No money.'

Boys walked backwards on the path in front of her.

'You-me-taka.'

'I have no taka,' Maggie said.

A boy took hold of her left leg as she stepped towards him. Another wrapped his arms about her right.

'Taka,' they said.

Hands closed around her belt, others around her ankles.

'No taka,' she repeated, and pretended to walk on.

Her legs were locked in their clutches. Tiny fingers and palms feathered a cushion that took her weight as she fell. Her heels lay on the dust path, while her body and head dropped gently to settle on the grass.

With a shriek of tiny voices, the children were gone.

From her back Maggie admired the blue of the sky. She sat up and saw the lawns with adults at a distance, and the line of trees that bordered the pool. She reached up for one of the combs knocked out of place in her fall.

A girl watched her, huge eyes peering round a tree trunk. Legs and arms, bodies and eyes sprouted from behind other trees.

The girl stepped fully into view. Her dress was dark red beneath its coating of mud, sleeveless but with a white trim to the hem and armholes. She was barefoot. Her dark hair was thick but short.

'Here,' Maggie said, and held out the comb.

The girl stayed still.

'Here,' Maggie tried again. 'I have no taka. No money. Take this.'

The girl stepped forward. Her bare feet crossed the stones on the path and she held out her hand.

Maggie pinned the comb straight into her hair.

The girl froze, as though any move and the comb would fall. The laughter of the other children relaxed her. She took the comb out and examined it, running her fingers along the bleached bone curve of its spine then rippling them along its teeth.

The children circled back around Maggie as she stood up. She took the other combs from her hair and planted them in the heads of different children.

'There,' she said when she was done. 'No combs. No taka. Nothing else.'

The children stayed. They were looking up at her hair.

She held out one long strand that had tumbled to hang across her shoulder.

'My hair? Is it funny?'

She examined the strand herself. Its pure white was striking. Lovely against the dark green of the tree. The blue of the sky. She churned the whole mane of hair with her hands then flipped it forward to hang as a curtain before her face.

'Boo,' she said, and stared out through a gap she pulled apart with her hands.

The children shrieked and stepped back a pace before the first ones chuckled. Soon the chuckles grew into laughter. She repeated the trick.

'Boo!'

I've become a mad old woman, she thought.

'Boo!'

I shall collect stray cats, live in a caravan and wear cardigans with holes.

'Boo!'

The laughter lessened. The chuckle died from it to be replaced by shouts. Her act had changed from a game to a challenge.

The first boy stepped up to tug at her hair as she parted it.

'That's enough,' she decided, but couldn't just walk away. The humour had turned. There was opposition between herself and the children once again.

'Give me your hand.'

The child didn't understand, but soon she had his hand in her own and another to her other side. Through a mixture of gestures and manhandling she arranged all the children to stand in a ring.

'Keep holding hands,' she corrected the first couple of times as the circle broke, and soon the ring was firm and she was leading it through steps and a la-laed tune that switched to singing as they whirled round and round.

'Ring a ring of roses,' she began.

'A pocket full of posies
Atishoo, atishoo
We all fall down.'

She slowed the last words, raised her arms to signal the drop, and as she stopped skipping the children tumbled around her.

'Let's try again.'

They laughed, and reassembled.

'All fall down!'

Some had learned the prompt. Others just copied and fell.

'All fall down!'

The tune of the song was hummed around her.

'All fall down!'

She heard the occasional English word.

'All fall down!'

It was a general shout. They raised their hands in the air and bumped down on the grass together.

'Bye bye,' Maggie said, when this latest bout of laughing was done.

She stood up, brushed down her skirt, and raised her hand again.

'Bye bye.'

'Bye bye,' the tiny voices repeated. Their hands clasped and unclasped to copy her.

It was a new game.

'Bye bye,' they said, and scattered around her as Maggie headed for the gate.

'Bye bye,' somewhat louder, the call mixed with words of their own.

'Bye bye!' the final shout, as fists punched the air in salute.

Maggie stopped at the other side of the gate to wave one last time. The children were already running off to some fresh game of their own.

* * *

'Ayeeeeee!'

The scream started high and whooped higher. It came from below her. Maggie couldn't look and see, because she was falling. Looking backwards at the children in the park, she had failed to notice the life out in the streets.

The sky flashed between the wings of crows, grey birds with black hoods, whose talons just missed her face as they were shocked into flight.

She had backed into a body. It was as low as a child's. Maggie fell beyond it. Her landing was soft.

The scream gathered fresh breath.

'Ayeeeeee!'

The crows cawed and voices jabbered in a world abuzz with noise.

Maggie stayed silent. There was nothing for her to say.

She was the sane element in an insane street.

The woman trapped beneath Maggie's legs pulled herself free as Maggie looked on. Her right hand pointed at Maggie. Her fingers were splayed, forking the lightning of her anger.

The lady was small. The only movement was of her mouth.

A tawny brown cloth was wound tight around her body to form her dress. It stretched over her head to frame her face. The skin was thick, whorled with lines from her forehead through her high cheekbones, as though whipped into being by the eyes.

The eyelids snapped shut for a moment and Maggie noticed the mouth. The tongue was grey. It flicked out the last of its words but the sound had already left, and the lady's jaw sagged.

Maggie patted her sides with her hands, feeling herself into shape, trying for ways to appear less frightening.

She could see what she was resting on now. A hessian sack.

'Is this yours?' she tried.

The lady blinked at Maggie's speech. Her mouth closed to moisten itself then dropped back open.

Maggie stood up and hoisted the sack upright. Much of its contents had spilled out. Paper and cardboard littered the ground by its opening.

'Is this what you were doing? Collecting the garbage? It's lucky it was so full. It gave me a soft landing. Were you bent over it? Is that why I fell over you?'

Maggie stopped speaking. Her small-talk exhausted, she made do with pulling the mouth of the sack closed and tipping it toward the lady.

'Sorry,' she said.

The lady jumped forward to take hold of it.

Maggie noticed an empty cigarette packet on the side of the ditch close to the park gates. She fetched it and dropped it in the sack.

The lady stared at the contribution, then up at Maggie. The eyes were less fierce now. A smile touched her mouth.

'You do a very good job,' Maggie offered. 'There's really not much rubbish left to find.'

She walked back along the ditch to a candy wrapper and a couple of pages of newsprint lodged beside the park railings.

'There you are.' She dropped the paper in the sack and clapped her hands to clean them. 'That's everything straight. No harm done.'

The lady's mouth opened, but wide this time to show her few pointed teeth, and her voice shouted out in a laugh. It was as high as the scream, but more staccato.

Maggie looked around. She was a drama with spectators. Passengers watched from rickshaws that ringed the scene and blocked the traffic.

'Rickshaw?' one of the drivers asked. Maggie recognised his tangle of beard. The man wouldn't take no for an answer. He had turned round to wait for her exit from the park. 'Want rickshaw?'

The lady swung the sack across her right shoulder. She looked up and spoke but Maggie only understood the leathery hand that closed around her own.

On the whole she was content to be led away.

* * *

They came to a large traffic island. The traffic kept to the wider roads that led off it, but they walked down one that soon became no more than a lane. Maggie had been checking the position of the sun to keep some sense of direction, but the shadows lengthened and the lane became so narrow the sun didn't touch her at all.

Her spine ached as she straightened herself with another bit of paper.

'Enough!' she declared, and waved her hands to show she had stopped.

The lady nodded, her speech interlaced with chuckles, hoisted the sack onto her back, and was gone. Sudden speed whisked her round a corner. She reappeared as Maggie stood still, beckoning her on.

Maggie walked forward and turned the corner. Beyond it were doorways, strange shops, and a display of uncomprehending faces. The woman had disappeared. Dim light bulbs hung from long flexes in darkening rooms. Their light did nothing to show Maggie the way. She began to hurry on to nowhere. It was better than turning back. She had taken the inhabitants of these lanes by surprise. Her appearance stunned them into tableaux of their lives, their conversational gestures frozen in mid-air as faces turned to watch her pass. If she turned back now, they would be waiting for her. The flip-flops thwacked against the soles of her feet as she shuffled into a run.

Houses to either side were squat and square, the white plaster of their walls both stained and peeling. Travel is romantic when conceived of at home. It's a dream. Travel in reality is the stuff of nightmares. Maggie was pushing an aching body through a stench of cooking, of kerosene fumes from stoves, of raw sewage, of sweat, smells flowing through this channel of sordid lanes.

She didn't belong. Such was the simple fact. She wasn't poor. She wasn't needy. She was English. She had been bred and trained to grace an estate, to take tea in rooms with vaulted ceilings, to stretch her gaze across distant horizons where green fused with cloud or occasional blue. Being lost in these lanes was like being stuck in someone's throat. She was alien. She was an obstacle. She would be swallowed whole or spat out.

Maggie was not tall, but she had stature. She realised that now, raising her head and pulling her hurried feet back into a steady walk. This was just another garden party she was required to attend. It was the equivalent of her annual appearance at the dinner dance to raise funds for the British Legion, of which Charles was the patron. It was the Armistice Day service in the village church of St Jude's. It was yet one more occasion in which she walked proud just so she could walk through it.

Her pattern when moving through such ordeals was to look straight ahead. Slowing her speed let her look to her side, however, and what she saw slowed her still further. The run of bare and functional buildings was replaced for a moment. The front of this new building rose through three floors. It had the grandeur to be a palace on this tiny little street. The rooms inside extended out through rounded balconies, so that the façade was a gallery that opened the palace onto the street. Wooden panels carved into delicate trellising completed the arches of every door and window. The wood was painted the blue of a soft pale sky, while the walls shone white. They reached up to a series of short towers, each one capped with a bulbous cupola shaped like a turban. From inside Maggie heard the sound of running water, and imagined a fountain splashing in the centre of a marbled courtyard. She kept moving, seeing nothing through the fretwork of the lower windows but breathing the clean air from inside. The tales that caught her as a child were not those of the Brothers Grimm, they weren't the perils of young lives in northern forests. She entered the fantasies of *The Arabian Nights*, tales spun by women in sunlit and starlit rooms. This house was a palace spun into reality from that world. It dwarfed her to the size of a girl captured by wonder.

'Tssss.'

The lane ahead turned round the side of the palace. The old lady, bowed beneath her sack of paper, stood at the corner and hissed between her teeth. Her hand flapped like the single wing of a bird, urging Maggie to keep up. She turned and shifted down the lane and out of sight. Maggie walked more firmly but was tiring of this game. A bell rang, a bicycle bell, set to come around the corner from the other direction. Maggie had learned how to place this sound. It would be a rickshaw, and ringing for custom. She would wave it down and it could carry her away.

She paused to let the bicycle appear round the corner, then turn and come towards her. The driver was straining too much to see her, standing to press his weight and knotted muscles down on the pedals. Maggie started to raise her hand to call him to a stop, but left it suspended halfway as she stepped to the side. This was not what she expected.

The rickshaw carriage was missing. A low cart was attached in its place. It moved on two bicycle wheels, but as they revolved to smooth the cart above the surface of the lane a wider movement spread to the cart's sides. The cart was narrow, yet women surrounded it to span the whole lane. Their legs beat inside the cloth of their saris as they ran. The saris were of plain cotton, once coloured but washed and scrubbed and beaten into greyness. The women's faces were ashen too, shadows overlaying and dimming the brown of their skin, faces made gaunt with masks of grief. The driver kept pressing his finger on his bell, whoops and wails spinning high from the women's open throats as they packed the street behind him.

It wasn't a race, for no woman tried to get in front of the driver, but a group from the back kept running up the sides to press their bodies in and reach the front of the cart. Those at the front let themselves be eased back towards the rear, their arms stretched out, their fingers clawing for a touch of the bundle on the cart even though the contact was no longer theirs. These circling women were the true wheel that drove the cart, the driver pushing and pushing to keep himself beyond their reach.

Maggie would have moved out of the way, but the lane was filled and she had nowhere to move to. The women who surged up the sides from the back tangled their legs with hers, pushed her with their arms, an urging of flesh on flesh and bone on bone as they carried her with them to reach their goal. A woman turned to face her as she failed to budge, her eyes flashing from grief to blame, the wail of her cry breaking into a stab of insults, fingers reaching in between Maggie's ribs to wrench her to one side.

Maggie tried to spin clear but the press of women wouldn't let her. She was pushed up against a woman who was reaching into the cart. As this woman was pressed back toward the rear Maggie's legs were shoved up against the cart's wooden side. Hands pushed at her spine to buckle her forward. The bundle in the cart was wrapped in dark grey blankets, but feet appeared at one end and a head was left clear at the other. The women were mourning the corpse of a man. Maggie's head was bent down above his face.

A grey beard tapered from his chin. His mouth hung open to show four yellow teeth. His eyes bulged open and wide but didn't see her.

An arm pulled Maggie away, the press of bodies turned her round and round, and then the women and the cart and the corpse were all gone. Maggie turned the corner and kept on walking, but did not notice where she was going. She was still looking down into the man's dead eyes. Those eyes were as clear as in a black and white photo, a picture of the moment of his passing. The dead eyes were not vacant. They were etched with fear.

Charles's eyes had been closed when she came to find him. Flick then hid the closed lids behind sunglasses. The eyes she had seen, the dead man's eyes, were the eyes of Charles. Of Chumpers. She had been made to look into them at last. She had seen the fear he felt at his death.

Let me out of here, she thought. It was a thought, not a prayer, for she had nowhere to direct it. Let me out of here and I'll remember you, Chumpers. I'll scrape up fond memories and grieve a little. I'll feel sorrow for your fear. I'll see you out of all this.

The lane ahead was sealed by another squat white house. The old lady had disappeared down some new turning. Maggie was lost, but as she resumed a steady pace her senses came back. She remembered a trick from when Mawsby still had a maze growing in its gardens. A sure way of finding your way to the centre, then out again, was to follow the right-hand walls. She did so now. The lanes grew narrower but she was on course. The road turned again and she met the sky.

It had darkened to a rich blue, streaked with red and amber. Across the road the solid buildings had gone. Dull lanterns illuminated low huts, flimsy structures made of wood, bamboo, tin and reeds. Small patches of orange burned near the ground.

In front of them stood the lady with the sack.

She beckoned Maggie toward the flames of the encampment fires.

* * *

A siren blared. It marked the end of the day's fast. Figures that were crouched around the first few fires reached out to receive cups and plates.

Maggie's path was a passage of darkness threaded between the embers. Fires scraped into the ground lit the immediate ring of faces but no further. By the broad white opening of a hut a few rows in, the sack of waste paper had been lowered to the ground. The lady's hand flew wide to point her out, then accepted a few bank notes as a man focused on Maggie's approach.

'Good evening,' he said as Maggie stepped in front of him. 'You are English?'

'Of course.'

His cheeks fleshed out as he smiled.

'You are helping our friend. She is very clever. She waits for *Iftar*, the end of our fast, then brings us her sack. We must give her food when she arrives at this special time. You will join us.'

He backed through the doorway. Two oil lamps behind him reflected off columns of paper wedged between the earthen floor and the ceiling. The columns at the front were of uneven height. They formed seats for three men who looked down at her while bundling rice from tin plates into their mouths.

Her host settled himself on a canvas stool, and pointed her to another stool set against the outer wall of the hut.

'Please,' he said, then switched to Bengali to snap commands into the darkness.

'What do you do with all this paper?' Maggie asked.

'We buy it. We sell it. We give two taka a kilo. It is something. A little help.'

He beamed his condescension down at the old lady who sat cross-legged on the other side of the door. Her fingers twisted some rice on a plate into a small ball. The old lady looked up to collect his smile before pushing the rice into her mouth.

Maggie stiffened her back to raise her height a fraction above the man's.

A small boy ran in with two tin plates. One he gave to the man, the other to Maggie. It contained rice and a side-helping of chickpeas in a yellow sauce.

'We are poor people. Very poor. But we give what we can. You would like a spoon?'

He shouted at the boy who ran off.

'He is ignorant. He does not know. He brings us spoons now. And drink.'

Maggie was left to wait and smile back. This was her old forte after all. She was a professional social smiler.

'This is China,' the man said, introducing the first of the men on the paper columns. 'His grandmother was born in China. This is Africa. His uncle is African. And this is Kung Fu. A Kung Fu expert.'

Maggie nodded back at each man. They were ranged according to size. China was the slightest, and sat on the highest stack. The other two men were both lean, but Kung Fu was noticeably the larger of the two. He sat on the lowest column.

'And this is Australia,' Kung Fu announced of her host.

Australia was a Buddha in his fatness. The thin blue lines of his striped shirt were sucked into the folds of his flesh. His hair grew long at the sides but had slipped from the dome of his head to leave it sweaty.

'Why Australia?'

'He has a visa,' Kung Fu explained. 'We all try. He gets it. He goes next month.'

'For a holiday?'

Kung Fu translated her question and the others laughed.

'I have a contract,' her host explained. 'For work.'

'What do you do?'

'There I am a cleaner.'

'Offices?'

'Sewers. I will help clean Australia's sewers.'

Maggie set her mouth back into its smile. The boy hurried in with two spoons so she had her food to play with. He set a bottle and two glass tumblers down on the ground, then ran back outside.

Australia kept his spoon heaped and his mouth full. His tongue rolled rice back toward his throat. Grains slithered from a corner of his mouth as he spoke.

'You are thin. You must eat.'

She separated the food within her mouth so she could swallow without chewing.

'Why do you come? You are with an NGO?'

'I don't think so. What are they?'

'Non-governmental organisations.'

'No.'

'Then with the government?'

'No.'

'You will have a new government in the UK. There is an election soon. Everything will change.'

'I don't think so. People vote for what they've known. Not for change.'

'Your Conservative Party is rich, no? I would vote for rich people. Rich people do not need to cheat. Your husband is rich?'

'My husband is dead.'

'You are a widow?'

He finished his meal, licked the tip of his tongue round his lips, and translated the news for the others. The lady in the corner laid down her empty dish, freeing her hands to express what her speech could not. She held them to the sides of her head then shivered them down to the ground.

'Our friend is a widow too,' Australia interpreted. 'She knew you are alone. Rich and alone. You are old. Very old and wise. Your hair is the colour of clouds, white clouds that hide the sun but give no rain. She is happy to bring you here. I am happy too. We will drink together.'

He spoke in Bengali and the three men dropped from their paper columns, taking the lamps with them as they stepped outside. One lamp was placed outside the doorway to light Australia from below. The angle of light left Maggie sitting in shadow.

'I must go.'

'You must stay. And drink. The others go. Drinking is forbidden. It is not good they see us. But our old woman stays. You are not alone. And the drink is good. Rice wine. Not strong, but very good. Here.'

He poured a few inches of wine between the two tumblers and handed one to her.

'We drink to your husband.'

She touched her lip to the glass but took in nothing.

'Your husband was a bad man? You will not drink to him?'

She tipped the transparent wine into her mouth. Much of it was water. The taste behind it was musty but fairly sweet. It went down without burning. As she bent forward to set her glass back on the ground the alcohol lifted through her head.

'I must be going.'

'Why? Someone waits for you?'

'It's late.'

She checked her watch.

'What is the time?'

'I don't know. I couldn't see my watch. It's dark though. I have to go.'

She stood and moved into the light of the doorway. The three men hadn't moved far. They stood in a semi-circle with their backs to her, just a few yards away.

'It is a pretty watch. It sparkles. But it is not good for you. It is too small. You cannot see it.'

It was true. The face was tiny, buried in a diamante strap. Maggie could not recall where it came from, how much it was worth. She clasped it on each morning, a habit she carried with her.

'Perhaps I can find one. A big one. For you to buy.'

'I have no money.'

'But in your hotel. You have money in your hotel. Your family has money.'

'I have no family. I am alone.'

'Then why hurry? No one will miss you. And you have those bangles. They are gold, no?'

Five thin plain bands hung on her right wrist. Her hand had stiffened with age. She could no longer bunch it small enough to work the bangles free.

'They're stuck. They won't come off.'

'We will cut them. Cut them off.'

'I must go,' she said.

The three men faced her now. She fumbled at the catch on her watch strap and pulled it off.

'Here.'

She bent and pushed back the tawny cotton of the old lady's left sleeve. The watch swung round the thin wrist when she snapped it in place, but it didn't matter. She doubted the lady would keep it for long.

Instead of the bangles she offered Australia her hand. He closed it in the flesh of his own and held it there.

'Thank you,' she said. 'You have been very kind.'

He stared at her in silence for a while.

'Yes,' he finally admitted. 'I am kind. I can be kind. Next month I go. I leave all this. This month is Ramadan. A holy month. You may go.'

He pulled his hand back.

'Go home, lady. You do not belong here. You know it, we know it. Other guests we have like you, they do not get to go home. We are poor, lady. We cannot afford to be kind.'

Maggie didn't look back. If men followed her, she would know it soon enough. The best she could do was step on in her darkness.

A choice of rickshaws waited on the street. She selected one with a light flickering from its wick in a glass jar suspended beneath the carriage.

'Hotel Solub?' she asked.

The driver was in his forties, with a trimmed grey beard and red scarf tied around his scalp to trail down his back. He stayed on his seat and stared at her.

'Hotel Solub,' she repeated.

He nodded and climbed down. As she settled in the painted carriage he drew the hood above her head. Her blinkered view was of his narrow body rising and falling on the pedals, and at times of the men he stopped to speak to.

'Solub?' she heard him ask.

The men shook their heads and peered round the canopy to stare at her, or spoke for longer and the rickshaw turned round. They were lost. They rode along broad streets and tucked themselves through narrow lanes.

Maggie recognised nothing. Tiredness stroked her feet, something between a warmth and an ache. It mingled with the rice wine, still releasing its vapours into her system. She wondered how far the effects would spread.

* * *

The driver held her wrist between his thumb and forefinger and tugged at her arm. Maggie woke and blinked at the fluorescent light from the hotel foyer. She stared at the driver's mouth, fascinated by the stumps of his teeth. He was demanding something of her. She presumed he wanted his fare.

She climbed down.

'Excuse me!' she called, and the hotel owner turned from the TV set in the corner to regard her. His chair swivelled to make the movement easier. He claimed to have a degree from the London School of Economics. He could make use of it now, by sorting out the rickshaw driver's fare.

'Please pay him. My money is in my room. I don't know what he wants. Pay him whatever. I will pay you back.'

The owner stared at her, then signalled the driver to step forward. He reached into the wooden drawer of his desk and pulled out a ragged banknote. The driver took it and departed.

'Ten taka,' the owner told her. 'I will add it to your bill.'

He took out a pencil, sharpened it, and added the sum to a page in his ledger. The exertion sent sweat streaming down the rounds of his face.

'You look wan,' he told her. The quaint perfection of Bengali English surprised her, with its preservation of antique words. 'Please, please use my hotel. It is not good for a woman to go out alone. Especially at night. You want something, we are at your service. I will have it brought to you in a jiffy. You are the guest of Hotel Solub. Let us honour you.'

'Sepen? Is he here?'

'He is sleeping. There is another boy on duty.'

'No no, that's all right.'

'You want only Sepen? I understand. Go to your room. I will bring him to you.'

'There's no need. Honestly. I'm quite tired. I'll just go to bed.'

'Then he will come to you there. Whatever you want, Hotel Solub obliges. We are your home far away from home. A discreet family hotel. Five minutes, and your Sepen will come.'

Good, she thought.

CHAPTER 8

H E KNOCKED ON HER DOOR AND CAME IN. Such a child. She was a mother, a grandmother. She should really be visiting him, telling him words of bedtime comfort, singing a lullaby, tucking him in.

'Hello, Miss Maggie.'

It was a sleepy voice, a sleepy smile. His hair was brushed, and he was wearing a fresh shirt that came down to his knees, white and striped blue, the neck open so the bedroom light warmed his dark throat and dropped shadows toward his chest.

He looked so tender, so beautiful, that tears gathered in her eyes. She decided to let them flow.

'Miss Maggie? What is the matter?'

'Nothing, Sepen.' She wiped her eyes with her hands, and decided to stop crying. It was too soon to lose herself in this young man. 'I'm just tired. And pleased to see you. It's been a long day. And dangerous I think. I'm not used to your country. Come, sit down. Just for a few minutes. I need to talk.'

She patted the end of the bed, and held out her bottle of duty-free scotch. He wagged his head to decline, and sat on the bed so gently it barely moved beneath him. As she poured the whisky into a tea-cup and sipped from it, he turned his head away.

She admired his profile. The nose she already knew well, that smooth line from his brow, but there was this smooth run from his nose to his upper lip to appreciate too, and the quiet chin beneath.

And then his neck.

She could imagine herself a potter and shaping such a neck, the ring of her hands rising to build it round and straight, with the little knob of his Adam's apple pressed out by her thumb.

She would choose a clay the dark colour of his skin, a clay with some gold shining beneath its surface.

'You are a woman,' he complained, and turned to face her. She saw that he was blushing, that his face burned. 'Why do you drink?'

'Because I'm a woman.'

It was a silly response. The drink was talking, not her.

'When I was a little girl I didn't drink. There was no need. It tasted horrible, and my body had enough to do simply growing. I see children now and feel so sorry for them, with all that growing to do. Imagine it. Bones and flesh all stretching, stretching. If it happened overnight, think of the agony. That agony is stretched all through childhood. It's an awful thought. Awful.'

Maggie paused to shiver at the notion, and took another sip of scotch to warm herself.

'Then we're all grown up and learn to like the taste of drink. Perhaps for the burning it can give us inside, the way it can lift our heads off, as though we're still growing. That could be so, don't you think? I think we grow nostalgic for our pain.'

She drank again, to feel the whisky coursing through her.

'I've done other things to my body. I tried anorexia for a week but tired of it. Sex with my husband was dull too, though it made me pregnant of course. I didn't drink then. A baby kicking the lining of my stomach while the stomach grew was enough. That's why we drink, Sepen. For the comfort of the memory of pain.'

'Drink is bad,' Sepen insisted.

'Maybe I'll stop when I'm truly old. When my body starts shrinking. Do you think that's a painful process?'

She finished her whisky, and curled her arms around her legs. The bed made a very narrow world, but she could think of nothing beyond it that she wanted. Sepen faced her, sitting behind his crossed legs.

'Let me tell you of my day,' she said, and told the story to bring him up to their present moment together.

'You are drunk, Miss Maggie. Those are bad men. They give you rice wine. It is strong. It takes your sense away. That is stupid, Miss Maggie. Very, very stupid. You are lucky to be alive.'

'I know.' She reached forward and patted his bare ankle, holding it for just a moment before letting go. 'Lucky to be here on my bed and talking to you now. Enough about me. How was your appointment at the airport?'

'The appointment is with a plane. When one flies in, I am there to meet it. Like I met you. Today there is no one.'

'I'm sorry.'

'Four times today I take the bus to the airport. I find no one.'

'You work hard. What do you do for fun? What do you enjoy?'

'I do not enjoy.'

'But you must.'

'You fill a lady's sack with paper. It is adventure. You want no money. I fill a sack with paper. It is work. I want six taka.'

'But you can't work all the time. When you are not working, what do you do?'

'I sleep.'

'But you must do something for fun?'

'I sing,' he admitted.

'Sing for me,' Maggie asked. 'Please.'

He looked at her. It was a gaze more than a stare. She was comfortable looking back. He sucked in his lips to moisten them, and his song began.

The language was his own. She watched his mouth form the shapes of the words and studied the emotion in his eyes. With his back straight, his body was an instrument that produced the tune. The voice was pure, and though pitched as an adult sound it lacked vibrato. The song collected beneath the net canopy of her bed till it was finished.

She let the silence gather a while before speaking.

'That was beautiful.'

'It is the song of my country. By Tagore.'

She reached down to the floor, brought up her bag, and took out her notebook and pen.

'Will you write it for me, please?'

'But you do not understand it.'

'I know it's beautiful. I would like to see it. To have it in my book.'

She moved round and opened the notebook along the edge of the bed. Sepen shifted himself to sit beside her. She watched his fingers curl around the pen, the movement of his wrist as he made his gentle strokes across the paper, the concentration that tensed the muscles of his eyes. His script was tidy. She liked the pattern of the letters, and the way they hung down from the line like bunting.

'Now I write a translation,' he announced.

The movements were less fluid, the concentration greater, but the writing was still neat. At first the letters hung from the line like his own Bengali, then they rose a little. He leaned back when finished, studied the effect, then looked across at Maggie.

'It is good?'

'Please read it to me.'

He read her the Bengali, then handed her the book.

'Now you. Read me our song in English.'

Maggie paused as Sepen did before starting his song. She wanted to read well. Then she began.

Oh! my golden Bengal
I love you.
Your sky – Your wind
Plays flute in my heart for ever.

Oh my mother! It charms me
In the spring having scent
From the new mango leaves.
Oh mother! What I saw
In the paddy field in Autumn -
What I saw —
That's a smile full of life.
Oh my golden Bengal
I love you.

Sepen laughed. The laugh was like several extra notes remembered from his song.

'It is lovely, yes? It is right? Everything is right?'

Maggie thought of questioning the verse as she spoke it, toying with the grammar. She was glad that she hadn't. Sepen's own words had come through her mouth.

'It is a lovely translation. It felt very good to speak it.'

'It felt good inside, yes? It is better than your drink?'

'It is good,' she conceded. 'Your poem tasted good.'

He laughed. 'That is funny. Funny English. Poems do not taste. Food tastes.'

'And mouths.' Maggie looked at his lips. Before they could lose their smile she leaned forward and kissed him. A light kiss.

Just moist enough to leave a taste.

'Thank you for coming. I know I woke you. You're tired. You've got a room of your own for the night. You must go back there now.'

Her kiss had removed a barrier, but there was still a distance between them. He must make moves of his own to cross it. His youth was delightful. It would be fun to watch him grow up.

He turned off the light as he went from her room, but left her door open a crack.

Maggie lay back, checked for any taste of his mouth on hers, and carried her findings into her sleep.

Postcard...

The first postcard Flick received from Dhaka showed a photograph of Brighton Pavilion:

I'm the ghost of Dhaka. Float around like a mad white thing.
Drifting by day, sweating by night. HOT BUT BEARABLE –
Maybe that can be my epitaph. Or is it too kind?
love,
Maggie
X X X

CHAPTER 9

SEPEN WAS IN THE BREAKFAST ROOM when she appeared.
'No planes to meet today?'
'I worry for you on your own, Miss Maggie. Yesterday is not good. I wait for you.'

'How kind.' She sat down, and waved him to the other chair at the table. 'So what do you plan to do with me today?'

'What you want, Miss Maggie. We visit your boy.'

'Not today. My boy is seven years old. That's too young for me today. I need someone with more experience. Someone who can teach me about your country. Tell me, what was your life like when you were seven?'

He told her of Paradise. Of a patchwork of fields that all reflected the sky, till shoots sprang up and the fields grew sturdy with rice. Rice plants so green you forgot you were hungry. Scents that floated and cooked on the hot breezes. Forests of purple shade, pools broader and deeper than the grandest of swimming pools in the finest of Dhaka's hotels. Bullock-cart rides to a phosphorous sea on a stretch of golden sand so long that no one has seen both ends of it on the same day. His childhood tales lit his eyes.

'And where is this heaven?'

'No heaven, Miss Maggie. Our heaven is not on Earth. But the green of the rice fields, that is the colour of heaven. Cox's Bazar is beautiful. Very very beautiful.'

'Cox's Bazar? It sounds English. Is it far?'

'A long way, Miss Maggie.'

'North or south of here?'

'We are in the south. Dhaka is south. But this is further still. South and south again. The end of Bangladesh. Nearly in Myanmar.'

'Myanmar?'

'Burma. A new name for Burma.'

'Then take me there, Sepen. Take me south.'

'When?'

'First I must have breakfast. Then we shall decide.'

She turned her head toward the kitchen.

'Tea?' she called. 'Whoever's out there, bring me tea.'

* * *

Maggie's suitcase was stowed behind her feet, her hands were held loosely on her lap, and sunlight dappled through the trees to fall upon her progress. She was being borne along a wide avenue, just a little slower than a royal carriage might do but as fast as the rickshaw driver could manage. To her right was a large sandstone building, with enough turrets and latticework to be a palace. To her left, cool and white beyond acres of tended lawn, was a domed building so large and pure it made Brighton Pavilion seem like a fairground mockery.

'The Law Courts,' Sepen explained.

'So much law and order in Bangladesh? You surprise me.'

They drove through the university area. Today it was closed. To Sepen it was a dangerous place. A student had been stabbed to death at the gates of the British Council just the day before. Mercenary thugs battled it out in front of the neighbouring Vice-Chancellor's house in aid of their political parties.

'What students do?' He held out his wrists, each so slender she could circle them with the fingers of one hand. She thought about trying. He took a finger and slashed across one wrist, and then another. 'They do this. With knife. Students of one party do it to students of the other. It is common.'

Maggie shuddered. It was hateful to think of men with knives. Of wrists being slashed. There was so much more a fine young man could do than wound.

'All students should pass an entrance examination,' she declared. 'In imagination. Politics and fighting, it's so ridiculous. Young minds should think of beauty, not pain. It should be required of them.'

There was so much that was beautiful. Maggie shifted herself in the carriage so that Sepen's body pressed against hers, and looked out. The grandeur of this part of the city was more comfortable for being faded. The walls of the streets were coloured with bright patterns of graffiti. It was leafy, shaded, warm and quiet.

'I like it here.'

The journey was a sweat for the driver, but then he was young and glad of the fare.

'You will like the bus, Miss Maggie. It is busy. You will be happy not to fly. You see life. See life, meet the people, and you will not be lonely.'

He was being silly. Life was deeper and harsher than that. But she found pleasure in his voice. It was youthful and floated, like a counterpoint to what she knew. His hip and shoulder pressed against hers. It all helped. She felt the strictures of her life loosen about her.

And saw a naked boy.

She spotted him while Sepen talked, and watched as he approached.

A thin strip of red cloth was tied around his forehead, bunching in his mass of black curls. There was no beard, though pubic hair was thick around his groin. Maggie guessed his age at sixteen. His penis was large and dangled as listless as his arms. Arms like on Michelangelo's statue of David, veins passing down them and along the hands, physical perfection to be admired. His chest was broad, his walk steady, bare feet padding him slowly down the middle of the road.

His eyes were like the statue's too. Maggie looked into them as they drew close but knew she wasn't seen.

'He has the eyes of a hen,' Sepen observed.

Maggie looked at him.

'They are spinning. He is mad.'

Maggie turned round to stare over the canopy at the retreating figure.

'You must not look.'

'Why?' The young man looked more like a child from behind. She didn't know why. The back was muscled, the buttocks were taut. Perhaps he was simply becoming smaller as the distance grew between them. Perhaps it was easier to look on as a mother than a woman now she was viewing from behind. 'Because I'm a woman?'

Sepen stayed quiet. She considered his reaction. She supposed it was due to some religious prudishness. Perhaps though he wanted her to look away from a naked man out of jealousy.

Perhaps both.

She smiled to herself and enjoyed the rest of the journey to the bus station.

* * *

The man's umbrella drew tight, fast circles near the ceiling of the bus. It was furled and black. In contrast the man's overshirt and loose cotton trousers were white, as were his long beard and the lace cap on his head. His body swayed with each swing of his umbrella, and his head tilted back. He shouted up into the face of the driver who stood beside his seat to shout back.

Maggie sat by the aisle in the centre of the bus as the argument drew others towards it. The front of the bus was a fury of language and flailing hands. Suddenly the old man walked towards her. He didn't smile, but his face was calm.

'What was all that about?' Maggie asked Sepen as the man settled down in a spare seat the other side of the aisle and the bus moved off.

'It is about dignity,' the old man turned to explain, in an English made somehow more precise by a high, needle-like voice. 'And respect. I believed when I was old that I could relax and enjoy my position, but alas. I have to work harder than ever. The young forget to respect their forefathers. I have to train them. You are English, is that correct? Tell me, what is the situation in your home country? Do you have respect now you are old?'

'I am not old,' Maggie informed him.

The man leaned across the bare metal floor. He wore pebble glasses but his eyes still looked small as they examined her.

'You are sixty,' he said.

Maggie said nothing, but her look of shock confirmed his guess.

'Ha! How do I know? It is my business. I have met westerners before. They travel so they can feel young. They say age is an attitude of mind. This is nonsense. Age is a process. I can read it in the skin. I am a doctor.'

He handed her a card. She read his name, Abdullah Ibrahim, and scanned his list of qualifications as he spoke on.

'They tell me I must buy a ticket. I ask them why. I have been working for more than forty years. They cannot know how many lives I have saved, how many of their cousins now live because I helped some far-distant cousin years ago. Now my own body is old, and I ask them to help carry it forward a few miles. They owe me so much. It is too little to ask.'

'Don't you have a ticket?'

'With my life. I have paid with my life. Now they call me "old man", and want a few taka more. Still, I have taught them. They know who I am. And you, dear lady. You are travelling alone. Where is your husband?'

The doctor looked down at the ring on Maggie's wedding finger. Her knuckle had swollen with age to lock it in place.

'My husband has died,' she told the old man.

'Then you are a widow,' the doctor declared, and smiled for the first time.

The smile showed her his teeth, pointed and marbled with yellow, and she smelled the breath that gusted between them. 'I too. I am a widower. It is a big world and we are so small within it. Perhaps Allah decrees that we are to meet here and now.'

Maggie turned to Sepen.

'I'm doing it,' she said, and pulled a face that only he could see. 'Seeing life. Meeting people.'

'It is good, no?' he asked, then gave a laugh that she thought might see her through.

* * *

A series of bridges, recent gifts to Bangladesh from Japan, let the Green Line bus ride above the rivers that crossed the early part of their route. Then the wide roads narrowed and the bus chugged through traffic towards its first ferry, parking near the river bank to wait its turn to board.

'Stay here,' Sepen informed her. 'It is best. I will go. For a minute. It is time to pray.'

The bus emptied itself of all but Maggie. The driver stepped out with his plastic bucket, gathering water to fill the radiator tank that was set beside his seat. Many passengers simply retreated into the shadows thrown by the shuttered teahouses. Sepen followed Dr Abdullah Ibrahim into a raffia hut set aside as a mosque. Maggie was small inside her bus, as the bus was small within its line of painted trucks, but still she was plainly visible. The first child found her within a minute – barefoot, brown shorts, red singlet, tousled hair, large brown eyes, a bottle of Pepsi in one hand and the hand of a tiny girl in the other, who held out the bottle opener.

'Pepsi,' he asked. 'You buy Pepsi? Ten taka.'

As he spoke the bus filled with other children, carrying bottles, pitchers of water, boiled eggs pushed forward in a nest of a napkin, short fat cucumbers and a knife to peel them, a bouquet of four cigarettes.

'No,' Maggie said.

Empty hands reached out for her money.

'Ramadan,' she tried, as if fasting, and motioned with her hand across her mouth that she could neither eat nor drink.

The children were laughing now, piling onto the seats behind and beside her, reaching over her head and up from the floor to float their goods and hands before her eyes.

They were no threat, she told herself. Only children. Scores of children. She could not buy from all, she had so little small change, so it was best to buy from none.

'No,' she shouted.

A bunch of bananas was lowered into her lap over the seat in front of her. The bunch was as broad as a young boy's chest. She stared up at the boy as she felt inside the pocket of her skirt for her single small banknote. With a twist of her wrist she wrenched two bananas loose. Her other hand offered up the bank note. It was for five taka.

The boy's mouth opened in a howl of disbelief. Tears coursed down his face, leaving clean tracks in the dust on his skin.

He flicked at her note with his hand, dismissing it as he shouted and cried.

'More?' Maggie asked. 'You want more?'

She dared to bring her purse out of her bag, pressing open its clips.

'I don't have small notes. Can you get change?'

She held out a hundred taka note. The boy didn't even see it. At a loud male shout from the front of the bus the crowd of children thinned and scattered but still the boy stood there, holding the bananas against his chest, wailing out his curses.

The driver stood in the aisle. The boy flicked a hand at Maggie and screamed his grievances. When the driver took Maggie's five taka note and held it out the boy ripped it from his hand, screwed it into a ball, and tossed it on the floor. The driver picked it up and lifted the boy beneath his other arm. The boy was tossed from the lower steps of the bus, still crying, the bananas held against his chest as his free hand checked his fall. Another boy collected the banknote the driver threw down and stood by the boy's side.

'Pepsi?' The tiny girl held out her bottle opener.

Maggie handed the boy and girl a banana each. They looked puzzled, then grinned, worked their way round her knees and ran off down the bus.

Passengers reassembled on the bus before it drove on to the ferry. The doctor leaned across the aisle as she finished telling her story to Sepen.

'My dear lady,' he addressed her, and pulled a white handkerchief from a pocket to mop the tears from her cheeks. There was something mesmeric in his eyes as they looked through his bottle-lens glasses at her. His gaze, and his touch through the handkerchief's cotton, left her strangely soothed.

'We are alike, you and I. I saw the boy. I saw him spit on your money. It is good. You teach him a lesson. He learns some dignity. There are greater values than money.'

'I didn't want his bananas,' Maggie complained. 'I didn't know I wasn't to break the bunch. I didn't know what they were worth. I wanted to do good.'

'Ah!' the doctor exclaimed, and settled back in his own seat as though a grand truth had been confirmed. 'This is the sadness of the West, this wanting to do good. I am a doctor. I do my best, I watch people die. There is no room for sentiment in my work. I do not want to do good. I simply do it. It is an obligation. For you it is a game. I am sorry, dear lady. We cannot be idle in this country. We have no time for your games.'

The doctor closed his eyes. The young conductor rode the front steps of the bus and banged its sides, shouting out its destination as it rode the ramp and left the ferry to continue its southward journey. Maggie closed her eyes too, to remember the broad grey waters of this first ferry crossing.

Her mind flashed between pictures of the river and a small boy's tears, till eventually it sealed itself in sleep.

* * *

The range of hills to her left was burnished red as the bus hurried on, its horn blasting a path through a street that was already empty. Then it wove at speed through groups of people gathered as shadows in between the houses of a village, and jerked the passengers forward as its brakes slammed it to a halt.

The bus emptied itself. Maggie climbed out under a darkening sky and looked around for Sepen. He had wandered off into the crowd, somewhere between the lamplit stalls and groundsheets stacked with food. The amplified cry from the mosque stretched itself away from the village and across the neighbouring fields. Maggie heard the softer sounds of meat sizzling on coals, water falling from pitchers, and voices building up from the silence of people feeding themselves.

It was *Iftar*, the end of the day's fasting. Maggie smelled the feast in the air and wondered what was safe to buy for herself.

'Miss Maggie?'

Sepen stood before her. A mouthful of food passed down his throat. He licked his tongue around his teeth, smiled, then held out his hands. They were empty, just those slender fingers of his playing in the warmth of the air. Then the fingers of one hand rippled a wave, the hand turned around

110

on his wrist, and reappeared with its fingers bunched. The hand was no longer empty, but held a small banana as delicately as if it were a flower.

She watched his left hand, saw it ripple through the same operation, watched a second banana appear from nowhere. He bowed, holding out his gifts till she took them, then looked into her eyes as he straightened himself.

He waited for her smile. She gave it to him. He turned and carried it away, back into the stalls of food that somehow had plenty for all.

CHAPTER 10

A PLUSH NEW HOTEL GRACED THE SEAFRONT. It was a palace of marble, light and space. Its rooms were opened by security keycards, air conditioning kept mosquitoes at bay, the sheets were crisp, the soap wrapped. The toilets had seats, which were sealed by protective paper bands. The furniture was of pine and quite adequate, and the view of the ocean from the window was exotic.

The hotel's details were easy to imagine. Maggie had read about the place in a guide book. She wished to go there. Raw from endless hours on the bus, her body craved a hot bath.

Outside the bus the world was confusing. There was no pattern to the street lighting, just an orange luminescence from bulbs high up on poles and strung on wires, and the clash of neon from shop fronts and cafés to either side. Rickshaw drivers jostled to collect her bag from the roof, men pushed past her on the narrow strip of pavement, horns blew, dogs barked, and she turned from it all to keep her eyes on Sepen.

He handled the matter silently. His hands did much of his talking. They reached up and her bag was dropped toward them. He flicked his fingers through the air and a single rickshaw pulled up by her side. She climbed in beside him and opened her guidebook to read the name of her chosen hotel.

She could make out nothing. The rickshaw swayed with the tread of the driver on its pedals, and the patches of light that were strong enough to read by soon passed.

'The best hotel,' she announced. 'Tell him to take us there, Sepen. The very best hotel.'

'I know, Miss Maggie. We are going. This hotel is very good.'

She wasn't convinced. She angled her open book towards the neon lights from the shops and traced her finger down the page, homing in on the five-star name. She was very close when she heard shouts from up ahead.

It was a chant yelled out in a loud male chorus. The clenched fists of men's right hands punched the night, fists coloured orange by the flames of burning torches. The rickshaw stopped as the marchers parted around them. Some men glanced at her, others stared ahead. The heat of their torches passed Maggie in waves, like the touch of their anger.

'They are from Jamaat Islam,' Sepen explained. 'Our nationalist party. Very popular here. Today, one of their members is killed in the north. They are protesting.'

His voice was flattened from its normal warmth, a tone she hadn't heard before

'You don't like them?' she asked.

'I do not like politics. Allah belongs in the heart, not in the head.'

He clenched his fist and held it against his chest. Maggie in turn closed her guidebook and slid it into her bag. She didn't understand the mood of this street, but the principle of choosing her own hotel seemed less worth fighting for than it had.

* * *

The rickshaw pulled off the long main street and down a dark and dusty lane, then turned into a large courtyard. Flowers were fragrant in beds to either side. The rooms were set off open corridors on three sides and at three levels. These corridors were something like the verandas Maggie imagined in the homes on old tea plantations. That thought appealed.

Eager to be happy with the place, she found the traces of imperial glory in the dim and unattended lobby. The dirty walls were lined with embossed paper of the deepest maroon. Brass fans hung motionless from the ceiling. The staircase up from the lobby was wide, the banisters carved. She knew stately homes of friends in England which were grand yet as weary and dingy as this.

No single rooms were available.

'Just one double,' Sepen said. 'For the lady. I will get a cheap room somewhere.'

They inspected the standard of the room. Its luxury was in its size, a suite of three rooms stretching back from the front. Furniture was basic. Two padded vinyl armchairs sat in the front room, twin beds in the centre with their individual mosquito nets, and a table and chairs were set in the back. A shower room was walled off from that rear chamber.

'Too big for one,' Maggie declared. 'I'm not wasting my money on a separate room for you, however cheap. We shall share.'

She registered the shock on Sepen's face.

'We can move the beds. Put one in the front room.'

It wasn't possible without removing the legs. The base was too wide. Sepen hauled the mattress off its stand and through to the front room. He lay down on it and fell instantly asleep without the protection of the net.

Maggie laid herself down on her own bed and stayed awake as long as she could. She had hoped to be able to hear the sea from her choice of hotel, its waves crashing onto the sands of the longest beach in the world, but the sea was too distant.

Instead she listened for the softness of the breathing in the neighbouring room.

* * *

Morning came. Maggie lowered her feet to the bare cement floor and pined for luxury. She padded round to the front room.

The sheets on the mattress were straightened, and Sepen was gone.

It was too early to face a cold shower. Maggie put on fresh clothes and wandered off in search of the restaurant. Several white jeeps were parked in the courtyard, with UNHCR stencilled around a logo on their sides. A few westerners from relief agencies, attracted by the plight of the quarter million refugees from Myanmar now homeless in the south of the country, sat around the upstairs dining tables. Maggie was able to order a whole pot of tea instead of a sugared cup. She drank it, ordered herself a second pot, and ate poached eggs on toast. It gave her just enough hope to face the day.

* * *

The long road down to the beach squeezed itself into a walkway made from a latticework of red bricks. A woman padded barefoot along the path some way ahead. A fence topped with barbed wire ran to the right of the path. There were no airplanes but the grey runway and a control tower beyond the fence showed this was the airport.

To the left there was simply a wasteland. Small cows and a few goats wandered through the scrub, seeking out the tufts that clung to the desert. Ridges of earth and stone apportioned the land. They were too meagre to think of as fields. Maggie wondered how a country with the longest beach in the world could make so little of the fact. The place cried out for a row of beachfront properties, gleaming white with open aspects to the shore.

By a line of scrubby pine trees she paused for a while, glad to stand in their scraps of shade. As a backdrop to the sea they were pitiful. An avenue of date palms would give the beach a tropical fringe.

The sea was just a broad stretch of white sand away. A small village of beach huts lay to her right. She could not tell whether they were simply for changing in and out of wet bathing costumes, or whether these were rooms for those who rough their holidays in a Club Med sort of way. There were no open-air showers so far as she could make out, for rinsing bodies clear of salt between cooling dips in the ocean. She would investigate on the way back.

She took off her flip-flops and curled the sand beneath her toes. The turquoise band of sea was her target. The beach was hot. Like walking on coals. Maggie ran, hopped, took short steps then leaps, doing all she could to leave the ground but never enough to fly.

Instead she fell, and sat with her legs in the air while the sand burned through her skirt. Scrunching up the skirt she made herself a thicker seat as she fitted on her flip-flops, shook her feet clear of sand, and stood up. The beach burned through her rubber soles. She looked up to see the sun directly overhead. The sea still called her, but the protection of the pine trees was much nearer. She took a tentative step along the sand, walking on its fire.

'Miss Maggie!'

She turned to see Sepen jumping down from a rickshaw.

'Miss Maggie,' he said, and waved to her. 'Come. We are going to my village.'

* * *

Sepen had bought tickets for the short bus journey. The rickshaw took them into town, and the bus carried them just a few miles out of it. They climbed down onto a narrow road.

A broad path branched off it, a ridge of earth piled high to divide the fields. There was room for them to walk side by side, but Maggie was content to follow as Sepen led the way.

'You see those trees?' he said, and pointed to the edge of a forest far away. 'They used to be here. I can remember them. Now they have been pushed back. It is all fields.'

The fields were brown and dry, awaiting the waters that would see them sprout rice.

'But you can smell them still,' Sepen noted.

Maggie copied him, facing the forest and closing her eyes to breathe in. A fragrant breath of trees touched her face. She turned back to Sepen, and saw a small white paper kite in the distance beyond him, riding high on a hot current of air, its string leading down to the left of a farmstead. Their path ran straight and long towards the arched gate in its walls.

Sepen opened his eyes and noticed where she was looking.

'That is home,' he said. 'They will give you tea.'

He got excited as they drew closer, skipping forward then hurrying back to walk by her side for a few steps. At some sound she hadn't heard, though she saw him lift his head and poise for a moment, he ran off.

'The singing pond!' he shouted.

He was squatting on the bank when she came up beside him.

'Frogs,' he explained.

Black bubbles in the water, like crotchets splashed across a musical score, croaked notes that danced above them in the air.

Sepen's face was as peaceful as in his sleep. He stood and they both gazed into the pond then out across the land.

'There were trees around this pond too,' he said. 'I played in them.'

Some trees were still bunched inside the farmstead's walls. The walls were crumbled in sections by the trees' roots.

They walked through the gates. Maggie followed Sepen through the trees, their slim trunks smooth and grey, their sparse leaf cover mottling shade upon the path.

'Here it is,' Sepen called back. 'The swimming pool.'

Its water was a grey shaded green, like the woodland. Maggie stood beside Sepen at the top of the stone steps and looked down. The bottom of the pool would be thick with mulch.

'There are four,' he said. 'Four swimming pools.'

They were places where people bathed and washed clothes, where the infant Sepen splashed about.

'I will show you. We will have a tour. But first we must go to the house.'

* * *

The main building was ranged along a broad forecourt of orange dust. The forecourt acted as a playground. As Maggie and Sepen stepped across it, small children hurried in through a small gate in the surrounding walls. They kept at a distance. Some ran to stand below the run of the far veranda, others took shelter on the other side among the fringe of trees.

'They don't get many visitors,' Sepen explained. 'They're afraid.'

He didn't seem too confident himself. They approached the right-hand section of the building whose doors stood open. He asked her to wait on the veranda while he went inside with the news of their arrival. She watched him walk through the first room and disappear into the back of the house.

The walls of this front room were painted blue but otherwise bare. The cabinet by the far wall caught the little daylight that filtered inside, glowing on the ribs of a scalloped dinner service made from translucent salmon-pink china. Propped up next to the china were two brass light switches, made shiny with polish, though Maggie saw no sign of electricity in the house. Two simple chairs were tucked beneath a plain wooden table. Another table with cutlery drawers served as a desk. The large oak frame of a bed completed the furniture of the room.

Maggie turned back to face outside.

Some children were a few feet away, but shrieked and ran off as she turned. She watched and tried to smile, but was truly weary of such children's games. As the bolder ones began to take on the dare, scuttling across the dust towards her before running back to safety with squeals of laughter, she retreated into the house.

* * *

'Did you find anyone?' Maggie asked when Sepen returned.

'Auntie. She is making you some tea.'

'The house feels abandoned.'

'There is only Auntie here now. The others come and visit but live in town. They need the electricity and the telephone, she says. She does not know why electricity is so good. She is old with no electricity all her life. They can do the same.'

'But this was your home when you were a boy.' Maggie clapped her hands together and brightened her voice. 'You must show me around. Show me your bedroom.'

'I did not live here.'

'This wasn't your parents' house? Where did they live then?'

'I have no parents.' He had already told her they were dead. Now he told her more. 'They are killed in 1971, after I am born. Auntie's husband died then too, in the war with Pakistan. A farmer found me. He brought me here. That is all I know. I left when I was very young.'

'Have you been back here before?'

He shook his head.

Auntie came in, a small woman with an old face and large eyes that stared without expression. She wore a white sari with a red patterned border that followed the wave of the shawl across her head. Maggie smiled and thanked her as a cup of tea was set down on the table. There was nothing for Sepen. The lady stepped back and waited for the tea to be tasted.

121

The children now shot regularly past the door, some pausing to skip a few steps of a grotesque dance. Maggie shifted her chair so that their game happened behind her back, and sipped. The tea had come in one of the salmon-pink cups.

With her back turned, the children drew closer. Auntie ran to the doorway. Her feet stomped, she shrieked, arms flapped, and the children scattered. Her final shout broke into a high laugh.

A fire was sunk into the earthen floor of a recess in the next room, the kitchen. An iron pot sat on a grate above the embers. The fire's red was bright and calm. Maggie stared at it while the Auntie focused on her and spoke with Sepen.

The word 'Memsahib' bobbed up on the flow of Bengali. Maggie appeared to this woman as some ghost from the British Raj.

Maggie gulped at her tea. In three sweet and sickening mouthfuls it was gone.

'Come on, Sepen,' she said.

She smiled and said thank you as Auntie stepped back to clear the doorway. Sepen's relief at being outdoors seemed as true as her own.

'Did she remember you, do you think?' Maggie asked as they headed across the courtyard.

'She is old.'

And I am possibly older, Maggie thought.

They followed the kids. These kids were like Sepen would have been, most likely, chased away from the main house if they dared to draw too close. He had possibly never

122

been in it before, not till he brought this strange white woman.

Beyond the garden wall were the earthen homes of the peasants who worked the land. Stepping through a flurry of hens, Sepen led her into an abandoned house.

'This is it.'

Feathers and the tar of chicken droppings covered a bench seat. The earthen walls were still solid, as smooth as expert plastering. Small patches of sky showed through the straw padding of the roof.

'The house I lived in. It is good, no? Cool. Cool in summer, warm in winter. Much better than the cement of the big house. My job was carrying water. We played over there.'

He waved his hand in one direction, but looked at the dust of the ground. The enthusiasm in his voice was forced. His songs of childhood were now laments to something lost.

He's growing up, Maggie thought. It was sad, for his youth and innocence were beautiful, but she was so far ahead of him in years and experience it did not really matter.

Some of the villagers called out questions to him. He gave the briefest of answers and walked away. The frogs were still singing as they headed back to the main road, but Sepen didn't turn his head from the path.

* * *

The sun had another hour left in it when they returned to the town. They moved from their bus to a rickshaw. Instead of heading straight for their hotel, Sepen directed their rickshaw to head along Sea Beach Road to the far end of the beach. A few couples and families had dressed up in their finery and come out to promenade. Small women in bold saris, broad wrappings of silk in bright blues, oranges, reds and gold all stitched with shiny thread, marched in silver sandals across the compressed sand. It smacked of liberation, Maggie felt, to step out so brightly at dusk.

A shy girl clad in black stood behind a red cart. The cart was metal, and sealed with a lid. Sepen handed her a banknote which she tucked into a recess of her clothing, then dipped a ladle into the cart's interior. It came out filled with hot peanuts, which she tipped into a paper cone. Sepen handed it to Maggie like it was a posy. The cone was made of newspaper. The curlicues of the foreign script were oddly attractive, but as the peanuts' heat seeped through the paper Maggie thought of the newsprint staining her hand. She supposed peanuts were safe, though was wary of street-bought food. She was doubtful of eating from paper – back home she knew people ate fish and chips wrapped in newsprint but it was an unfathomable taste. Here it seemed safe enough, she supposed, since the monkey nuts were baked in their shells. She cracked one open, placed it between her teeth, and tried to smile as she bit down. She had endured a full day in the sun. She was tired. Though once a dab hand at insincerity, she was finding it hard to be appreciative of this peanut gift.

She licked the peanut from her teeth, gulped the particles down, and spoke for want of sighing. It was an old habit, an old choice. One could wilt with tiredness, or rouse oneself and find fault. This was not a safe place in which to wilt.

'You do nothing for yourselves in this country,' she complained. 'Cox's Bazar. The name has so much promise, a mixture of England and the Orient. I'm told it has the longest, sandiest beach in the world. What did I expect to find on such a fabulous beach? Fish restaurants perhaps with lanterns and linen tablecloths and wicker chairs within sound of lapping water. Beachside bars with glass tabletops and chrome fittings. Freshwater showers to wash clear the sand. Beach umbrellas and cushioned sunbeds. They manage them in Greece. Greek travel brochures are full of them, and goodness knows Greece seems poor enough. What have you got here? A peanut vendor with her wooden cart. When you do build beach huts they have no facilities that I can see, and they back on to an airport. I ask you!'

'Beach huts? There are no beach huts.'

'At the other end of the town. Where you picked me up this morning.'

'Yes. They are new. Refugees live there. They come from Burma ten years ago. They live on the beach. The cyclone washed away their old homes.'

'The cyclone?' Maggie tried to recall some images from the television news back home.

'In April. Last year. Big winds. They pull the sea then push the sea into waves. Tidal waves. Waves as big as a house. A wave as big as a hotel. People are frightened still. Old people who live for ever, who see everything, say it was bad. As bad as they know and more bad than they can dream. You see those trees?'

He pointed up at the scrubby pines she wanted to replace with tropical palms.

'They are lucky. No branches now, but still in the ground. The wind pick up trees and whoosh.' His hands showed how trees were sent flying. 'A cyclone then tidal wave. A tsunami wave.'

They stepped up from the beach. Patches of scrubby grass studded fields that were baked between sand and mud. Scraps of bricks, slices of cement, coils of rusted wire, broken containers, a mess of industrial garbage littered the ground. As Sepen stretched his hand toward the area he conjured a different sight.

'Dead bodies. Everywhere. Men. Women. Children. Cows. Dogs. Fish. For days and days they come up from the sea. I watch it on TV. Bodies big with air and water. Dead bodies everywhere, like...'

He looked for words to describe it, then turned and pointed down to the ground and at the trail of shells she had left from feeding peanuts into her mouth. Maggie's fingers had broken through shell after shell, snapping them open and chewing the nuts down, all without thinking. The warmth of the roasted peanuts was pleasant as the sun burnt red and doused its heat in the ocean.

'Like peanut skins.'

Sepen looked from the wasted field toward the setting sun. Its reflection bronzed his skin.

'It is beautiful, no?'

'No. It's not. I'm sick of the sun.' She dropped her half-empty cone into a wire trashcan. A young girl in a simple brown frock ran forward from the gathering shadows and picked it out. 'My head is splitting. I've had too much, Sepen. Too much for one day. Take me back.'

She held out her hand. It was speckled, it quivered a little, but it was what she had to give. Sepen took hold of it and led her to the rickshaw. Maggie focused on the cyclist's taut calves as he churned the pedals to ferry them along the road. She did not want to know about the sea, the wasted field, or the bare concrete buildings on her right that someone presumably was proud to call home. She wanted to be back in their room. Her hand felt dry in his. Night fell quickly, a cloak she could hide her age inside.

'Cyclones,' she said, starting a list. 'Tsunamis. Earthquakes. Monsoons. Does it make you strong or fragile, living in a country that suffers so much?'

'War too.'

Maggie did not wish to think about war. Weather was safer.

'You would be cold if you came to England,' she told him. 'In winter snow covers the ground and turns everything white. Water drips from the eaves and turns to icicles before it can fall. Breath comes out of our mouths like clouds. Cold is our extreme. We do not have heat like you have here. We have warm, we have cool, and we have cold.'

She shivered, but not from thoughts of cold. She shivered at some shard of coldness inside her, that was yet to thaw.

The rickshaw turned into the driveway of their hotel and stopped just outside her room. Part of her could have wept at the room's bareness. Her body felt brittle. She needed to set it against a little luxury. Bathe it and wrap it in soft towels perhaps. Lay it onto a mattress that was firm yet forgiving.

Instead she would lie on her back, and ache, and wait for tiredness to wipe clear the day's memories.

'Good night Sepen,' she said, leaving him in his ante-room. The one comfort available to her was solitude. She would lie on her bed, close her eyes, and be neither seen nor seeing.

CHAPTER 11

'HOW ARE YOU?' SEPEN ASKED.

'How do I look? I'm fine. Perfectly fine. There's no need to worry about me, Sepen. No need at all.'

In truth, as she followed him on a tour of the town of Cox's Bazar, her insides were on a tour of their own. Bile collected in her throat and she swallowed it down. At times she paused to let dizziness fade from her eyesight.

They passed a Buddhist monastery, planted on stilts made of trunks of the thickest, darkest trees. A small temple behind it, white and with open walls, had a structural delicacy that appealed. Leaves cut from pastel tissue were strung across its ceiling like bunting, in strands spanning out from the centre. Stacks of bright paper flowers were wreathed around a golden statue of the Buddha. Should he become hungry, a plate of rice and chicken was set at his feet. Smoke curled up from sticks of incense toward the Buddha's nostrils. Maggie admired his stillness, and the contentment stuffed inside his cheeks. She would have liked to sit on the cool of the marble floor, face the Buddha and close her eyes till the day was safely passed.

Sepen led her on.

She carried her sandals in her hand across the temple's sacred ground, and followed Sepen out of the compound to a sandy path that ran up a conical hill.

'Do we have to go up there?'

'This is Jadi Pahar. Jadi means stupa. Pahar means hill. It is sacred. We go up for the view. I will show you the whole town.'

Maggie's feet scrambled for the toeholds that served as a path up the steep slope.

The hill was carved into a shelf halfway up, broad enough for a few palm fibre houses to stand there. Sepen had a chair carried out for her to sit on.

'Thank you,' she said. It took her a few minutes of sitting on the wooden chair before she was able to take in what she was seeing.

A small boy caught her attention, running barefoot down the hill with a blackened kettle in his hand. She traced his route ahead of him, the path forking across fields one way and through the temple complex the other, while her breath came back and her head was able to complete the journey her body had made.

A piebald dog ate rice from a tin plate. The pile disappeared till the creature was licking the final grains from the rim, chasing the plate as it span around and lodged against her foot. She followed a sound the other way to find some hens. They were cooped under upturned baskets and pecking at the bare ground. Then she looked at the people gathered to watch her.

'How beautiful these people are,' she said. Sepen translated and they smiled. She noted their golden skin, their raised cheekbones, and their grace of movement.

'They are Buddhists,' Sepen told her. 'Rakhain Buddhists. They make rice wine in the back of their huts and sell it. That is how they live. They say you are very welcome.'

She smiled back and pointed a finger at the faces of three young girls, where patterns glistened on their cheeks and foreheads.

'That looks lovely. What is it?'

The three girls hurried off, returning with a large black stone hollowed into a dip and a tablet of what looked like soap. They handed it to her.

'The pattern is made with sandalwood paste,' Sepen told her. 'It is cooling. Refreshing.'

'And pretty,' Maggie observed.

'They want to decorate you. Is that all right?'

The girls giggled and began rubbing the tablet in a few drops of water across the stone, grinding it into a beige paste, lifting glóbules of it on the end of a thin stick.

'You are hot,' Sepen interpreted, as the girls laughed at the touch of her face. 'They are surprised. They think white skin is cold.'

The fingers pressed into her skin, thin white lines that pulsed like veins across her face and allowed it to cool a little.

The boy with the kettle returned from the bottom of the hill. A couple of minutes later she was presented with a drink, in a cup of white china with a light blue rim. It rattled on its saucer, the surface of the tea shimmering as she lifted it to her lips.

'There is a stupa on top,' Sepen told her.

'What is that? What is a stupa?'

'A little white building. With a point on top. Holy for Buddhists. Not for me. The view is lovely from there.'

'Here is enough.'

Maggie looked left, to the clean lines of the five-star hotel that gleamed by the sea front, and then ran her eyes along the horizon. She had been up and down its long main street now and thought she understood the town, but from up here the street was lined in lush greenery as though it was primarily an irrigation channel for trees. The town was a narrow strip of concrete lodged in countryside. She followed the view of the sea round to where it met a broad river, and beyond the river a plain of fields that stretched towards a forest and far-away hills.

'You run up,' she suggested to Sepen. 'Come back and tell me what else you can see from there.'

He was enough of a child to go, the sand of the trail scudding up from under his feet as the girls ground more paste to wind a pattern across her nose.

* * *

They paused in the town to buy clothes, outfits of light-weight material for the steamy climate. Maggie rested on a stool and let Sepen perform the transaction. Her body ached on standing up.

From the main road Sepen led her through side streets, narrow ways blessed with shelter from the sun. Blind locals could find their way about by pushing their noses through all the different smells. They'd miss the pretty features though, the carved beams and trellised balconies.

Outside an old cinema a semi-circle gathered around an old man, one snake dangled around his neck while another raised its head from a raffia basket.

'My mother read me stories about snake charmers,' Maggie told Sepen. 'You're taking me back to when I was a little girl. I loved those stories from *The Arabian Nights*. Only now they're not stories. This is for real.'

The threads that held her to her old life were being cut inside her. She could almost hear them pinging loose.

They were too late for the fish market. A few unwanted silver fish slapped around on a couple of trays.

Severed heads of cows sat on butchers' stalls, their flow of blood soaking into the black wooden boards, all dreamy with their beautiful eyes.

'This is life,' Sepen said. He wanted to lead her into a small black hut set behind the row of butchers to witness the killing. It was the slaughterhouse. The smell of the blood was enough for her. The tendons in her legs turned to liquid and she was ready to buckle to the ground. It was only the river that kept her moving, the sunlight slashing streaks of silver across its surface, a light at the end of the walkway.

Sepen hired a boy and a boat and Maggie lowered herself onto its bench seat. The boy stood behind them and rowed a course in between fishing boats, wooden boats as dramatic as pirate ships with their bright strings of flags and high turrets set in the sterns. Boats that massed across the gathering dream that her waking life was turning into, and blocked out the light.

Maggie shivered. Ripples crossed the river from one bank to the other. Then their boat swerved. The boy steered them beyond the fishing boats and set them in the current. The town was behind them, the sea ahead. A flock of white birds studded a sandbank, specks of white in a band of gold beneath a sky of blue. Sepen laughed out and shouted and clapped his hands, to send the birds soaring into a white cloud, a cloud that fragmented into brilliant sparks as the birds dipped their wings into sunlight.

Maggie looked through them to the blue beyond, a blue that blurred in darkness at its edge until a black sheet gathered the colour into a single blot. Her body slumped from the seat. The cushion of Sepen's hand stopped her head slamming against the side of the boat. He cradled her in his arms. The boy pushed at his pole to urge the boat toward the nearest bank, shouting out for help.

CHAPTER 12

THE WHITE JEEPS OF THE UNITED NATIONS came and went in the hotel parking lot. They had arrived for the aftermath of the cyclone the year before, and returned in strength to administer the recent arrival into the country of two hundred and fifty thousand refugees from Myanmar. Sepen found a French doctor among a team taking lunch in the hotel dining room, and persuaded him to come and examine Miss Maggie.

The doctor was tall and lean, in his thirties, with his black hair combed back. A tie banded in different shades of green was knotted beneath the collar of his white short-sleeved shirt. Sepen waited outside in the corridor for the doctor to give him the news. He was glad of his daring in approaching a western doctor. A Bengali would surely have frowned, as though Sepen's attentions to the white woman were the real source of distress. The Frenchman was relaxed. He had taken a blood sample, but suspected amoebic dysentery was the principal cause.

'We can take her to hospital,' the doctor explained. 'But she is better here. You can stay with her?'

'Yes, sir.'

'Good. She needs care. This medicine will help, but your care is more important. She is lucky to have you.'

The doctor handed over the prescription, and checked that Sepen had the funds to pay for it. Sepen nodded. The doctor suggested how to treat the patient; cooling her with flannel presses, keeping bottled water to hand, holding her hand should the hallucinations return, moving on to spoonfuls of rice should she be prepared to stomach any food. Sepen nodded again at each new piece of information, then shook the doctor's hand before the Frenchman returned to his colleagues.

Maggie was asleep when Sepen returned to her room. He hauled his mattress back to the bed beside hers, sat on it, and watched the rapid breathing push against her chest.

She moaned. He stood and looked down at her. Her eyes connected with his for a moment before she rolled off the bed, attempting to stand then choosing to crawl, scampering on legs and feet to the bathroom.

It was a luxury bathroom, with a porcelain toilet bowl instead of a hole in the ground. She made it, and leaned her head inside. Heat and cold channelled around her body, fevers and chills fought to take hold, as liquid burned up through her throat and burst from her mouth.

There was relief. And a shaking that was fever and cold and fear combined.

'No!' she shouted, and reached a hand to push at the bathroom door. It was light enough to swing closed.

Sepen must not see her like this. This was not what she had planned.

She was in her nightdress. She had managed to put it on for the doctor's visit. Its white cotton was clean a few minutes ago. Now she pulled it over her head.

It was soiled. It stank.

What was the matter with her? Vomit, diarrhoea, both at once? It was impossible. Unmanageable.

She turned on the tap on the wall to fill an orange bucket, scooped water out with her hand to wash herself clean, then dumped the nightdress in the bucket to pummel it against the sides. There was no soap for the stains.

She needed soap for the stains.

Perfume for herself.

A bath with suds.

A bed with clean sheets.

Her body shook. She gripped the bucket for support. It toppled over but she held on tight as she fell back to the floor.

'Come,' he said. 'Come.'

Sepen had entered the bathroom. He tried to look away, from the first naked woman friend of his life. It was hard. She needed his help.

He wrapped a towel around her shoulders, and held it closed around her front with one hand. She looked away from him, her long white hair slick to her skin like the coat of a dog in a monsoon. He wrapped arms around her to stop her shaking. So frail, so light, hers was the body of a child. Light enough to move.

He stood, the lady hooked within his arms, and carried her to the bed.

'Stay,' she said.

'You are wet. I must dry you.'

'No. Stay. That's better.' And it was true. The room was so warm it was good to be wet. 'Hold me, please. Hold me.'

With her back to him, she pressed herself into the folds of his body. Her body soaked his. He kept his arms around her,

137

and as the shakes came back held her tighter. Give her care, the doctor said. It was good what he was doing. He closed his eyes, and held on.

* * *

Eyes of cows swivelled in the sockets of their severed heads. Snakes then writhed from the eyeballs, to be pecked in flight by hooded crows. Bells rang as rickshaws wove tracks around her. Faces leered in and swooped away. The shadows of children clung to her and smothered her, their voices crying and shrieking.

'No, leave the light on,' Maggie said as Sepen rose from the bed and turned off the switch.

She was not asleep as he thought, but only still. She closed her eyes, then opened them again as the hallucinations grew too vivid. Like the houselights in a cinema, the glowing lightbulb made the images fade away.

'But go. You go. You have to have your meal. I'll sit up till you come back.'

It was the last day of Ramadan. He had to eat before the sun rose.

'I bring you something?'

'No. Just bring yourself back.'

Once he was gone, she stood up. The movement prompted a wrenching ache in her guts, but she moved through it. Running a hand along the wall for balance, she walked to the bathroom.

The light was dim, but strong enough to show the shadows on her face. She was not shocked by her reflection in the mirror, but pity creased her. She leaned over the sink but there was nothing left to throw up. She was empty inside.

'This is it, Maggie.' The sound of her own name spoken in the night was strong. It called her to herself.

'Maggie,' she repeated more firmly.

She had no make-up with her. There was nothing artificial she could do to her appearance. No mask she could plaster on to hide behind. She was going to have to live with herself.

She had a small travel kit. Nail files, needles and thread, buttons, a comb, nail clippers. And a small pair of scissors. She picked them up and held them next to her hair. Slid a long white tress through her fingers. Snipped gently so that the hair fell one strand at a time to drift down and drape across her left hand. The cuts were close to her scalp. Cut by delicate cut she moved the scissors around her head, around and around as she watched in the mirror.

The person in the mirror looked dazed. She was remote. Maggie was cutting the hair of a stranger. She did so with a ruthless care. The woman in the mirror looked too old. Too tired. She needed renewing.

There.

The operation was complete.

Maggie studied her reflection. Closed one eye, then the other. Tried a smile. The woman in the mirror winked and smiled back. Maggie lifted the mane of her old white hair in her hands and pushed it against her face.

'Miss Maggie?'

Sepen had made his silent return. He stood in the bathroom doorway.

'Miss Maggie? What did you do?'

Her mind was far away. She dropped her fists to her breasts so the hair hung down to cover her naked body, and blinked at him. Tears collected in her eyes and dropped down but she was not crying. Simply in shock.

'Come, Miss Maggie.'

Sepen took her hand and led her back to the bed. In the world outside the cry to Allah was amplified from minarets, and daylight touched the windows. He took the bundles of hair from her and helped her into the bed, then covered her with the sheet.

She was crying now. She didn't know what for. Sobs caught at her throat. Each breath was short and hurt her, but the tears on her cheeks were warm. They moistened her skin and felt good.

She turned on her side and looked up. Sepen sat beside her. His soft brown eyes watered as he watched her. She reached up to touch his cheeks, stroked her fingers around the side of his face and through his hair.

'Sepen,' she said, and as she spoke his name she felt its power. 'Sepen. I love you.'

She curled her body round to bury her head in his lap, and shivered at what she had said. His body was stiff, the muscles tensed. Then he relaxed. His hand touched her shoulder, and then her head. His fingers discovered its new shape. Then his head bent to hers. His mouth touched the bare nape of her neck with a kiss.

* * *

'No, Miss Maggie. You sleep. It is Ramadan. Please sleep.'

She turned and pressed her back against him. He pulled away so that his erection did not touch her, but she reached round to draw him close.

'It's good. It feels good,' she said, and pressed her hand against his buttock to keep him there. 'Don't worry. I need sleep. I will sleep. But stay with me.'

He stayed on the outside of the sheet, but his arms came round to hold her. Sleep closed in as the sunlight brought pinkness and warmth to the room.

* * *

He was sitting on his own bed when she woke. She sat up, pulling the sheet to cover her breasts. A loop of orange beads moved around his fingers. His lips shaped the words of silent prayer. The lengths of her hair lay across his lap. He had braided them while she slept, a long white braid two inches thick.

As he looked at her, his lips continued his prayers.

She lay her head back on the pillow, and returned to sleep.

* * *

'You like to eat?'

'When you do.' She was awake again, but they stayed on separate beds. 'How long before you can?'

'Three hours.'

'I slept that long?'

'Yes.'

'And you were watching me?'

'Yes. You feel better?'

'I think so. Weak, but much better.'

'Then eat now.'

'No. When you do.'

'I will order it. Plain rice, the doctor says, when you can eat it. The kitchen is busy today. It is our holiday. Eid. Like your Christmas. The last day of Ramadan. Families buy new clothes and have a party together.'

'Oh Sepen. I didn't know. You must go. Enjoy yourself. Not stay with a sick woman. I am all right now. Please, fetch me my bag.'

He brought her the evening bag she had brought from Mawsby. She fetched out her purse and handed him some money.

'Go. Buy yourself some new clothes. Go and have a good time.'

'It is good here with you.'

'But a party. You have to have a party.'

'I stay here.'

'Then we'll party together. I shall eat my rice, and you shall have a feast. Please go now and order it from the

142

kitchen. Anything you like. Everything you like. But first, give me your shirt.'

He put his hand on the yellow shirt he was wearing.

'No, not that one. The other one. With stripes.'

He brought it to her. She put it over her head. It fitted her well. She and Sepen were matched for size.

'Thank you. Now please. I need this shirt till my nightdress is washed. Go and buy yourself something new. Do it for me. I wish to see you in a fine new shirt.'

He smiled, took the money, and left her.

* * *

Their food arrived on a trolley while Sepen was in the bathroom. The water from the shower ran over his head so he did not even hear it. Maggie walked to the door, gave a tip to the waiter, and wheeled the trolley through to the back room where she laid the meal out on the table. Her meal was plain rice in an earthenware bowl with a pot of tea. A separate salver of rice was for him, with a large plate of curried fish, some dhal, and a slab of naan bread.

He stepped out of the bathroom, dressed in his close-fitting black trousers and new shirt. It was purple with threads of silver sewn through it. She wanted to laugh when she saw it, surprised at his taste, but managed not to.

'Wonderful. So handsome.'

'And the food. This is very good.'

The table was between them. He looked at the food, and she at him. His hair was now longer than hers, and stuck up from how he had rubbed it dry. He was shy of her, and hungry. Shyness and hunger. It was what youth was about.

'When can we eat?' she asked him.

'They bring it early. We must wait. For sunset. For the call.'

They sat themselves down. Maggie took the lid off her pot of rice and placed it over his fish, to keep it warm. They sat silently for ten minutes while the light filtered out of the room. The speakers from the minaret crackled, then a voice called out across the city. The call to prayer of this first muezzin was soon joined by a chorus of others.

'Excuse me,' Sepen said. 'First I must pray.'

He moved to the front room. She saw his bare feet through the door as he knelt down. It seemed wrong to stay at the table. She went to her bed and knelt beside it. She had not prayed like this since she was a girl, but it felt right now.

'Dear God,' she started, silent words in her head. She paused to see what it felt like, talking to God again after all these years. There was something there, some pressure on her scalp. She didn't know if it was a true response, but was encouraged to keep on praying. She held her hands palm to palm against her chest.

'Let me hurt no one. Let me act only from love and not from power or greed. Let happiness come, but at no one's expense. Let me be silly sometimes, but not stupid. Let there be time for new life before I die.'

She wondered if there was anything else she could add, but there was nothing. Simply this new love she wanted to express, but not in words.

'Amen,' she concluded, and went back to the table.

Sepen joined her some minutes later. Maggie leaned across the table and served a ladle of rice and a fish onto his plate, spooning on the sauce and a spoonful of dhal.

'God bless,' she said. 'Now tuck in!'

She mimed the fast action of a spoon, encouraging him to eat well. He laughed, dipped his fingers into his meal, moulded some rice and fish into one neat ball, and popped into his mouth.

She watched it pass down his throat.

'Better?'

'Good.' His voice was strong. He almost choked on his pleasure. 'Very, very good!'

He prepared another fingerhold of food, and looked at her as he ate it. She smiled back, and dared to eat a spoonful of her own fresh white rice.

* * *

With a cup of tea and six spoonfuls of plain rice inside her, Maggie recognised she was drunk. Her head was giddy, her speech a little slurred, her movements slow.

She put it down to recovering health.

'Sepen,' she said, wobbling as she stood and holding on to the back of her chair for support. 'Help me to the bed, will you?'

He had been playful, saying how good it was to eat again. Now he was concerned as he hurried to her side.

'Don't worry. I'm fine,' she said. 'Lie down.'

It was her turn to take care of him now. The bubbles and caffeine in his Pepsi had gone to his head and made him silly. He giggled. That was OK. He was young.

She undid the buttons on his shirt. Stretched her palms across his skin to push the material aside. Wiped the sweat of her palms across his chest and down his ribs.

The trousers were held by one small metal clip. She undid them, pulled down the zipper, and peeled back the cheap black nylon. He wore nothing underneath. She paused to admire him, stroke him, and play with the beauty that rested there. Sepen was so small compared to Charles, the only other man she had known, but this was so large. His penis throbbed and grew thicker to the touch. She stroked her hand through the curls of pubic hair around its base, licked her finger to moisten the pink tip, and dropped spit onto her hand to rub around the flesh.

His fingers were locked in tension, in fright. She eased them with strokes of her own, then carried his hand beneath her shirt. His fingers stirred, moved around her, as his arm and body shivered.

'It's all right,' she assured him. Her body was shaking too. 'It's all right.'

She moved herself above him then eased down, his penis in her hand and then inside her, little by little. Her mouth hung wide open as she gasped in air and went further, took him deeper. Then she rocked a little, rode a little, contracted her muscles to clasp him tighter, relaxed, clasped again.

The whites of his eyes shone in his dark face. He cried out and pressed his hands about her waist and squeezed. His fingers dug into her flesh as his buttocks pumped beneath her. There was warmth, a spurt of saving warmth inside her.

She leaned forward, kissed his brow, played her fingers lightly through his hair, then lifted herself from him.

He was still half dressed. She peeled the sleeves over his shoulder and pulled the shirt from him. Drew the trousers down over his legs and feet. Sat beside him without touching for a moment, simply wondering at the dark beauty of his youth, the slender limbs, the gloss of his skin, the play of muscles beneath his flesh. Then she drew off her own shirt, lay down beside him, and pulled him close to her.

'Wonderful,' she said, and held him till his tension melted. 'My Sepen. My dear. You are wonderful.'

There was a knock on the door. After a few moments, it repeated itself.

'The doctor,' Sepen said. 'He says he will return.'

'Don't worry. I bolted the door. Tonight I need no doctor. I have my medicine.'

She kissed his shoulder. He held still for a while. As the doctor knocked one final time, she felt the muscles tighten in Sepen's back. And then relax. He spun around to bury his face in her breasts, to muffle his laughter.

The doctor's footsteps trod away. Sepen lifted his head and looked at her. There was playfulness in his eyes.

She held him tight and turned so he was on top of her, her head on the pillow.

'God I'm happy,' she shouted out on a breath.

It was as much of a prayer as the moment needed.

* * *

He was asleep, she was awake.

She slipped into her flip-flops and wandered out of their room. She wanted to look at the stars and say thank you. And maybe ask for just a touch of forgiveness.

The courtyard was dark. She was the only person awake.

Herself and a rat.

It was walking across the angle near where the veranda turned toward the reception. Going so slowly she could kick it.

Was it blind?

Was it a rat?

Mawsby's rats were plump beasts. This was more like a mouse, grabbed by the snout and tail and pulled very hard till it became long. Long with a weasel body that sagged in the middle, and clumps of fur pushed up by scabs.

Maggie lowered herself to her haunches. The rat observed her. She saw the dark knob of one eye. The other eye-socket was sealed by an overgrowth of skin. Like a wink.

Maggie winked back.

The creature's head lolled on its elongated neck. It was tensed for moving. It turned and sauntered toward the stone railings of the veranda, and disappeared through a gap.

She had wanted the rat to feel her love, and walk towards her to be stroked. Such a thing would be a miracle.

Instead she left the space beneath the stars and went back to her room. Sepen's arm lay above the sheet. His hair flopped across her pillow. He was wrapped in the softness of sleep.

How many miracles did a woman need?

She sat and watched him, and noted the occasional flutter of air through his lips, the flicker of dreams behind his eyelids. She leaned forward sometimes, holding her nose just above his flesh, gathering in the salted sweetness of his smell. When daylight came she would stroke him awake, and do her best to store in her memory the sense of touching him. She would kiss him, and collect the taste of his mouth and his skin. She was letting him go even while she was gathering him in.

Sepen. She mouthed the word. He would live his own life but she could carry his name away with her. She would have to leave this night behind, she was wise enough to realise that, but its memory could belong to her future.

She would wake him soon, look down on him, and memorise the brown of his eyes.

CHAPTER 13

MAGGIE WAS STARING OUT AT THE SEA through the plate glass window, so did not see the French doctor approach.

'Miss Maggie?'

She blinked up at him, then turned her head to check the rest of the room. Many other tables of thick clean pine stood empty. Apart from the waiters stationed like shadows around distant walls, she was the only customer. Surely this man could sit elsewhere. But he knew her name. That was a puzzle.

He smiled. 'Serge,' he said, and held out his hand. She lifted her own but left it limp as he pressed it. 'I was your doctor. I am afraid I only know you as Miss Maggie.'

'Maggie will do.'

'The young man is not with you? Your attendant?'

'He is at Biman. The state airline. Collecting my air ticket for tomorrow.'

'So you're leaving us. I'm glad you feel well enough to travel. I have ordered a coffee. May I join you?'

He pulled out a seat and settled himself down at her table before she could nod her assent. She had headed towards the sea to be alone for a while. A whim had brought her to this newest of hotels, to sit and be served afternoon tea in the luxury of air-conditioned surroundings. This café filled a section of the lobby, a cavernous space in which white marble reflected light. Maggie had thought she wanted to be alone, but as a waiter brought the doctor's espresso on a tray she saw that this was not so. She was simply preparing herself for a return of loneliness. She did not mind this young doctor's company at all.

'I've visited you,' he said. 'I knocked on your door but it was locked. Nobody answered.'

Maggie had nothing to say, so just smiled and took a sip from her cup of tea. It had grown cold. She had been sitting alone for a while.

'You look well,' he said.

Maggie looked down at herself. She was wearing her strand of pearls. She had placed them round her neck before stepping out on this trip toward the shore, like a thread of her old self that might lead her back to Mawsby. She fingered them as she spoke.

'Does an oyster think of a pearl as a gallstone?' she asked.

It was one of those stupid questions that idled through her brain now and again. The doctor's look of surprise brought her back to her senses, and she laughed at herself.

'I'm sorry,' she said. So much of her life Maggie had forced conversation out of herself in social situations, when she would much rather have remained quiet or walked away. It was her default program, now rusty through lack of use. 'It's a stupid question. It's the bane of doctors' lives, I suppose. Everyone you meet feels the need to bring up a medical enquiry. I've been staring out at the sea, and dreaming about when I was young. It's brought back a memory. I had a neighbour as a child who disappeared to hospital and came back with his gallstone in a jar. It was curious, but not valuable. If gallstones were as valuable as pearls, people would be killed for them.'

The doctor smiled, but out of patience rather than understanding. She noticed his eyes move to take in the state of her hair, and moved her hands up to press into its chinchilla softness. It was a tiny head, like the statue of Stravinsky's she had seen somewhere, with the same button sticky-out ears but without the brains. A dizzy head. She had let herself act like a teenager over these last few days. It really was time to shake some sense into it.

'Will you let it grow again?' the doctor asked.

Wisps of hair had dusted the shining scalp of Maggie's mother as the old woman lay dying. The touch of her own hair brought the mother to mind, leaning back into a bank of pillows and gasping dry-mouthed at the world. Maggie's mother had died too young, but already old. It was so simple to let yourself become old. So ridiculous to try back-pedalling into youth. So impossible. Like an inveterate non-swimmer suddenly deciding she could crest the waves.

'My hair's too white,' she announced. 'Black's not the colour of death. White is. My hair was too white and too long. There was too much of it.'

Her hair was like a shroud, a jet stream to send her heavenwards. The face of Sepen had made her mind how she looked. Within her illness she once popped out of her body to imagine Sepen's view of herself. She saw her ghostly face on its mass of white hair laid out on the white cotton sheets. Back inside herself she looked up at his eyes, at the darkness there and the way they shone, at the dark rings of his sleeplessness and the gold-dark skin of his nature.

She was whiteness and he was dark. She chose the dark. There was more love there. She cut off her hair.

She had found the hair, plaited and coiled and tied with one of her own dark blue ribbons, stowed away in the bottom of Sepen's bag. It was a worry till she asked. She thought it was kept out of sentiment. He told her it was for selling to wigmakers.

'You frightened me,' the doctor said. 'I see death and I see illness, but you were apart from that. You had a fierce will to live. Everything white, in this country it is shocking to see, but the circles of your eyes became black. Black and still, and focused, focused.'

She thought he was wrong. She thought she had been lost, not focused.

'Maybe the effect came from your hair. In bed your hair was volcanic. But now the hair is gone I look into your eyes, and they are the same eyes. The same eyes now as then. Wild eyes. Wild and focused. You are a wild woman.'

'You make me sound French.'

'Oh no. It is too easy to be French. French women are born to it. You are a wild Englishwoman.'

It was a compliment, but she did not care for it. It was too like a cartoon for an identity. She reached out to wave a waiter to come and collect the money for her tea.

'You are not white now,' Serge said, more to comment that to reassure her. 'You have the sun in your face. Golden brown. And your clothes are stunning.'

'They are not my choice,' she said, and felt somewhat guilty for the denial. Sepen had led her to buy clothes on their second day in town, two pyjama suits known as *shawal kameez*. Her own choice had been of material in black and silver but he had laughed her into buying this outfit too, and another in bright tangerine. Her legs were now in twin cocoons of a virulent pink, her top a strident orange. She had put the outfit on for this last day to surprise him.

To surprise the world.

To surprise herself.

'It's so very not my choice.'

She stood so the doctor could take in the full effect of her clothes, and laugh at her if he wanted.

'It is a new taste,' he suggested.

'Exactly,' she said, and picked up the suitcase that held the rest of her possessions as though the last word had been said. 'Good taste is a dungeon in which we hide ourselves away.'

'Have you changed hotels?' the doctor asked, surprised at the sight of the suitcase. 'Are you checking in?'

'No, checking out,' Maggie said. She laughed as though she had told a joke, and held out her hand. The doctor stood, and she squeezed pressure into their goodbye handshake.

'Thank you,' she said. 'You kept me out of hospital. I don't need institutions just now. You let me feel young for a while. I've been weak, I've been stupid, but it's not been bad. So I thank you.'

He watched her walk across the shiny floor towards the hotel entrance, and ordered himself another coffee. Taking

Maggie's vacated seat for a better view towards the ocean, he was able to catch one more sighting of her. She was carrying her suitcase towards the shore.

* * *

A fisherman entered the brown shallows of the sea, his dhoti pulled high and tucked in at his waist to form bulging swimming trunks. His dark body was knotted tight with muscle. Curls of black hair hung past his shoulders, and his uncut beard was twined to press against his chest in one long strand. He surged through the sea, his hands raised high and chest thrust forward at the waves, to reach his nets that were staked between poles to catch the tide. She loved the way his legs powered him. It was possible to walk through the waves. The ability to swim didn't seem vital at all.

The fisherman's catch swam in a tin bowl sitting just above the waterline on the beach. Maggie peered in at the darting specks. Fry the entire day's catch and it would make a decent appetiser at Wilton's, Winston Churchill's favourite restaurant on Jermyn Street that Maggie made her own on her occasional luncheon trips to London. She presumed these fish would provide the day's protein for the man's entire family. Sepen had told her more about these people by the shore. The man was one of the Rakhain Buddhists who lived in the rattan huts further down the beach. They once had lived in simple houses. The tsunami had swept them away. They moved closer to the dangers of the sea, not further away. Their homes were made of fibre, palm fronds and bamboo and were built on sand. They had no land. They lived on fish.

Sepen had told her more about the previous year's tsunami. In 1971 war had ravaged the country. Twenty years later cyclones whipped up tides and floods into a natural disaster. It was April 29th. This sea of soft warm water rose into a wave some twenty-five feet high. This tidal wave stretched the entire length of this world's longest beach and still further both north and south. It snatched island communities from existence and carried coastal dwellers inland to dump them like flotsam on hilltops, all in one forty-minute swell and rush and retreat of crashing sea. Cyclonic winds and rains battered survivors. They pulled through the wreckage of timber and stone, searching for their homes and their families. A hundred and thirty-eight thousand people were killed.

'How come I didn't know about this?' Maggie wondered. 'Why wasn't I asked to help?'

'This is Bangladesh,' Sepen said.

It seemed like answer enough, but Maggie wanted more so he tried again.

'Look now. Look today. Look south. We are a very poor country. But people come from Myanmar, quarter million refugees come, and we say welcome. We don't say go home. We say we have nothing, and we share it with you. In Bangladesh we have nothing, but we share it like we are rich.'

'But I didn't know. It was a tragedy and I didn't know.'

'It's OK,' Sepen said. 'You see Cox's Bazar. We have no tourists here. No English people died. Just Bengalis. Why should you know? But you are here now. It is good.'

Maggie stepped down to the edge of the sea. A jellyfish bubbled up from the shallows, an enormous grey bubble, like something Neptune had farted in a bath. It rolled forward with the lick of each bigger wave. It had to be dead, Maggie thought but didn't know. The sea was a mystery to her. This whole country and its people were a mystery to her. The more she came to see of it, the less she understood.

She turned her attention to the slope of hard sand. It was scored with intricate patterns, circular mazes built around a central point. She guessed that crabs had left the designs. The mass movements of these creatures were as bizarre as any she had seen. They raced as pale shadows across the sand, creatures of identical pace and direction, darting the swiftest movement and then suddenly stopping.

She watched a larger crab sink into sand that was touched by the sea, the stalks of its eyes looking out at her till the last moment before they too disappeared. This sand sucked at her feet as she walked, but her tread still seemed to shake the earth. The ground bubbled with crabs that had submerged at her approach, while others scooped sand backwards to dig themselves down.

Another crab, the size of her fingernail, stayed rooted where it was. Its rear was anchored in the sand while its pincers pulled at the side fin of a fish. The fish was about two inches long but a whale compared to the crab. It sat dead but

157

fresh, grey with a white mottled back and yellow eyes, untroubled as the crab stuffed its flesh into its mouth.

A wave came and tumbled them both apart.

The same wave lapped Maggie's feet.

* * *

Maggie stood on the damp and cooler part of the beach and set her suitcase down on the burning sand that lay just above it. She took out a T-shirt, in simple black with white daisies stitched around the neckline and sleeves, and laid it to the left of the suitcase. To the right she laid a plain white blouse. A bra went to the left, another to the right. She paused a moment, then selected two pairs of plain, dark blue knickers. One right, one left.

This was a ritual, but one performed with the simplicity of a children's game. In a similar way she had once arranged her dolls' wardrobe across the eiderdown on her girlhood bed. The doll lay naked in her cot. The clothes were the range of her possibilities for the day.

Now Maggie was being her own doll. She had brought along all her belongings. Everything that might contain her, might define her on this journey of hers, was packed into this case. Out came a pair of socks. To the left with one of them, to the right with the other.

She looked up. A boy and a girl were running along the shore toward her. The boy was pulling a cart along by a piece of string, but its wheels did not roll. Instead it tumbled and dragged along the sand. She guessed the boy was about five years old, barefoot and dressed in just a pair of red cotton shorts. The girl, most likely his sister, wore a plain light blue frock, the twin plaits of her hair bouncing as she ran. Maggie stayed where she was, kneeling on the sand, but stopped her ritual unpacking. She prepared for the company of children.

The symmetry of her task was obvious. The children understood it at once. The boy placed his cart higher up the dry sand, then both children bent down to the work. The case was like Noah's Ark. Everything had gone in two by two. Now their job was to bring them out again, moving objects to each side so as to form a long line of belongings, until the case was empty. The oddments came last, Maggie's towel at one end of the line and her toilet bag at the other. The boy reached into the toilet bag, eager to separate the soap from the shampoo, the eyeliner from the tube of face cream, but Maggie shook her head and indicated that he should just lay it down. She unstrapped her sandals and handed one to the boy, the other to the girl. A sandal was placed at either end and the job was complete.

Since walking away from Mawsby Hall with nothing but her evening bag, the clothes she walked in, her watch and bangles and ring and string of pearls, Maggie had enjoyed the idea of having no possessions at all. This line of belongings showed how foolish the idea was. She had done nothing but accumulate. For the tiniest while she had been pleased with each thing, and had only bought what she felt she needed. Now everything she had was ranged along the shore, and what she needed wasn't among them.

Some British politician once staged his own disappearance, his clothes abandoned on a southern English beach. Perhaps that fed Maggie's sense of ritual, but she had already achieved that first step. She had staged her disappearance from England. Now perhaps she was washing England out of herself.

She entered the Bay of Bengal. Just a few steps, so that the waves lapped around her ankles and pulled away again. She would wrap herself in the softness of the Indian Ocean. This ocean had turned the known world inside out in the cyclone of the year before, and taken people from the land to fling them into the air. The breakers today were frothy and foolish things. No matter how high they grew, they always collapsed. Maggie could manage such beasts as these. The sea that sent people flying would be kind, surely, and allow a non-swimmer to swim.

The sand was sucked away beneath her feet, and Maggie stepped forward to stand on firmer ground. The sea smoothed up beyond her ankles and played with the pink pantalooned legs of her costume. It took some effort now, pushing against the depths, but effort wasn't hard, it was natural. Waves parted around her as she walked.

She bobbed for a while, the air caught in her top like an inflatable cushion, then a wave slapped her chest and pushed the wind out of her. She let it go with a cry of surprise that was almost a song.

She lifted her hands like the fishermen, and bunched her fists against the sky.

A wave reared higher than her face and she jumped. Just a few inches, springing from her toes. Inches or miles, the distance didn't matter. She had left the earth. How she soared. She punched the air and her spine arched backwards, her very first dive and a pure somersault, through the white spume and into the greys and browns of blindness.

Her legs kicked, and her arms hit out against the water. A limb broke the surface and then her face, her nose and mouth. She drank in the air then spun round again.

There was no sky and no earth, no sense that she knew of, just this hurtling in between.

Without the panic she would be calm. It was that simple.

She gargled her scream for help

Her back pressed into the seabed, then her head, her body forced into a somersault while seawater flooded through her nose to reach around her brain. She was dropped onto her knees, her arms wheeled a perfect butterfly stroke upon the surface, her chin surged forward to burrow in sand, her hands pushed down to shove her forwards.

She crawled on till the sea had dropped back from her feet, and retched. Salt water poured from her insides to dissolve the geometry of the crabs' maze. The water soaked away and the sand was clear.

Maggie laid her left cheek onto it to rest.

* * *

161

She woke up with a wooden toy cart parked in front of her eyes. She followed the string the short way up to the hand of a small boy. He looked down into her open eyes while the sea pushed at her feet.

A girl's tiny hand pressed fingers into Maggie's left shoulder, trying to rouse her. She drew in her feet and sat up. The blue-frocked girl had been crouching by Maggie's side. Now she stood up and pointed down the beach.

The current had carried Maggie some hundred metres from where she entered the water. Back along the beach the tide was coming in. The boy and girl had rescued her belongings.

Everything was still in place in its long line to the right and left of the case, simply moved to dry and higher ground. The girl ran away and came back with Maggie's towel. Crouching low, she rubbed at Maggie's legs then stood to wind the towel around her waist. The boy ran up with a pair of her knickers in his hand. Maggie understood. She pulled down the trousers and her wet knickers, patted herself dry, then stepped into the clean pair. The girl ran off and returned with a skirt. It was an Indian cotton print, a swirling design of yellow and orange petals, one she had yet to wear. She pulled it on over the towel and tied it around her waist as the girl eased the towel away.

Then came the bra, and the plain white blouse. Maggie lifted one leg so the boy could slip a sandal beneath her foot, then raised the other. The girl ran off and came back with her brush and comb. Reaching high she stroked them across Maggie's skull where her hair had once flowed. The sun had blazed to a vast roundness, orange turning red as it dropped toward the sea. Just before it touched the horizon its bottom edge grew feathery, sinking into a band of distant cloud. A fishing boat passed in silhouette across it, like a pirate vessel with its pennant flags flying from the high wooden buttress of its stern. The sun dried the moisture from Maggie's face and crusted it in salt.

Her wet clothes lay on the beach at her feet, like a fluorescent snake's skin. The two children had packed the rest of her clothes away, and the boy dragged the suitcase toward her, churning a channel through the sand.

'Here,' she said, picking her wet clothes up from the ground. 'You can have these.'

The girl held out her arms as Maggie draped the wet clothes over them, but she did not smile.

'And the towel,' Maggie suggested, and draped it round the boy's neck. These were such feeble gifts, just her cast-offs. They had helped her far more than she was likely to repay them. They had helped give her back to herself.

Maggie opened the case and took out the toilet bag. The girl did not need cosmetics but this wasn't about need. She handed it over. And gave the brush and comb to the boy. Both grinned now.

'Bye bye,' Maggie said, and clasped and unclasped her hand in a childlike gesture of farewell. The boy ran away to collect his cart, then dragged it back towards her on the end of its string. The children lived here, she remembered. Their home was among the raffia huts on the beach. It was she that had to leave.

The sun was gone. She picked up her case and walked into the gathering darkness.

* * *

The outer huts on the beach were specked with the tiny lights of kerosene lamps. Maggie walked from the sand across the ridge where the few surviving trees still grew. Beyond them she looked for the end of the wide path of red bricks that was raised above the scrubland. It would lead her from the beach to the town.

The way was dark. The electricity supply was in a time of load-sharing, a power cut shifted around different sections of the city to give each home a share of what power was available. The foot traffic grew as Maggie left the beach behind her. Grey shapes of the tiny Burmese women brushed past her on their way home; a ringing bell announced the sudden approach of a rickshaw; a cow the size of a Great Dane weaved its slow walk around her. Maggie walked as far as the first road and set her case on the ground, waiting for the first empty rickshaw that might pass her way.

One pulled up in a moment, and its passenger leapt down. It was Sepen. He had come to find her. He took hold of her arm and helped her up into the passenger seat, then picked up her case and jumped up to sit beside her. She was not ready to talk. She managed a brief smile as tears brimmed in her eyes. They travelled in silence.

Maggie was starving. She wanted to say so but it seemed a little melodramatic in the context of Bangladesh where starving was too often for real. 'I'm hungry,' she said instead. They headed straight for the hotel restaurant.

Sepen poured water across his fingers and into a bowl, dried them, then reached across the table. His hand brushed her cheek.

It was a surprise. He was not confident about touching her in public.

'Sand,' he explained. 'Your face is stuck with sand.'

Her body itched inside her clean clothes, scoured in sand and salt.

'You are a crazy woman.'

He didn't smile. He was speaking the truth, and it disturbed him.

'I come back to the room and look for you, and you are not there. You are gone. Your clothes, your case, all gone. Then I find your bag, your passport, your money. You are a crazy woman. It is not safe to leave these things. I carry them when I come to find you. I carry your things and your ticket. Your ticket to Dhaka.'

Sepen had brought Maggie's shoulder bag along with him. It hung over the back of his chair. The noise of other eaters bounced off the white tiled walls, their tin tumblers clattering onto the steel tabletops.

'Did you open your envelope?' Maggie asked.

Sepen had bowed his head to his plate so that when he looked up at her she saw the milks of his eyes around the dark pupils. He carried on eating.

'It had your name on it.'

'I put the money back in your purse,' he said.

'Why? Wasn't it enough?'

It was a hundred pounds, two fifty pound notes. The amount was hard to judge – enough to seem handsome, not enough to spoil his life.

'How much would you like me to give you? Just tell me. Dhaka is no life for you, picking up tourists at the airport. You love it here. I see it in your face. I'll go to the bank in the morning. Take out more money. You can start a new life.'

'I want you to stay.' He tired of eating and cleaned his hand. 'I am a crazy man. I want to change life. Things come, things go. I want something to stay. I want you to stay. That is crazy. It's impossible.'

'The difference is too great. You are young, I am old.'

'No difference. You, me, no difference. We are same.' He reached into her bag, pulled out her passport, and opened it up. The mini coloured photo was of someone she had once been. Bones pushed paper white cheeks into shadows, white hair was coiled and pinned to her scalp, and her eyes were vacant. 'This is only difference. This is your picture. Not mine. I'll tear it up. Then you stay.'

He held his hands ready to do so. Maggie made no move to stop him. He tired of the pretence and slid the passport back into her bag.

'You play with me. Now you say the game is over. You are running away. OK. We have one more evening. We must eat.'

She watched him finger his rice into a ball and move it to his mouth. His tongue pushed inside the flesh of his lips as he cleared the rice grains from his teeth, ready for his next mouthful. He ate in silence, without looking at her. She watched him till she remembered her own hunger, then reached into the food on her plate to ball up a mouthful of her own.

* * *

'Why do you go for a swim? You cannot swim. It is stupid. You are sick.'

'It was an adventure. I like adventure.'

'But you cannot swim.'

'I went in the ocean. I came out again. Who says I cannot swim?'

Maggie was tired of replaying their argument. They were on their last rickshaw ride to the beach.

'Why do you take your case to the sea? With all your things.'

'I was going swimming. I cannot swim. I thought I might drown. I thought I might be swept out to sea and never come back. Fish would eat me. If that happened I didn't want you to have all the trouble of my clothes. I didn't want those things returned to my family in England. That's not how I want to be remembered. I left you some money in an envelope because I did not think you would take anything for yourself.'

167

'You go swimming and you think you will drown. That is so bad.'

'Do you know why I can't swim? As a girl I was afraid of water. I was afraid of many things. Nobody showed me how to overcome my fear. I was a girl. I was expected to be fearful. Nobody taught me to swim. I was afraid of drowning when I went into the sea today. I was prepared to drown, but I didn't expect to. I walked through my fear. If I can be terrified of the sea, yet give myself to the sea, and survive, it's a message from the universe. It means anything is possible. I gave my life to the sea today. It took it, and gave it back. Now I can do what I want with it. Anything is possible.'

'You are a crazy woman,' Sepen reminded her. He was still sulking. 'And you are flying away tomorrow.'

'There is nothing I cannot do. Nothing!' Maggie sang in response. 'That is the new song of my life, Sepen. Now it's your turn. You sing for me, please.'

He waited a while, still angry with the danger she put herself in. Then he sang.

It was a very moving sound. Maggie left the tears on her cheeks to dry in the breeze of the ride.

'That's beautiful. What is it about?'

'It is a song by Lalan. Five hundred years old but still true. The heart is a bird, the body is a cage. When the body dies the cage is open and the bird flies off. Where does it go? To the place from where it came.'

'You know some beautiful songs.'

'It is a sad song. Now we are together. But I go back to where I come from. You go back to where you come from.'

He sang to her again, his voice pure and surprisingly low. She asked for another translation.

'I sing of love. The pain of it is in the heart, like swallowed poison. When you reach for someone, there is only cold space for you to touch. Bangladesh is like this. We have great longings, but the only thing we have is poverty.'

'And your songs,' Maggie suggested. 'Who wrote that one?'

'It is mine.'

'You made it up?'

'I sing it. You hear it. And now it is silent. It is gone.'

* * *

They stopped at a run of brightly lit stalls at the end of a road that sold ornaments and jewellery, all made of shells. Maggie bought some souvenirs, then moved down the walkway and onto the beach where she sat and waited for Sepen to join her. He had a gift for her, but waited for the lettering to dry. It was a conch shell, banded in white and fawn. She held it to the lamplight and read its message.

For Maggie, with love Sepen

She cupped the shell in her hands so that its spikes pressed into her palms, and stared out across the sea. Sepen checked her face for a reaction then looked up at the sky.

'We go, but everything is here,' he said. 'The moon. The stars. The sea. The sky. Everything is from Allah. Thank Allah, and you will be happy.'

He sat apart as he spoke of his God, then reached for her hand.

'One more ticket,' she said. 'You can buy one more ticket. For you. To Dhaka. We can fly together. Have one more day. Would you like that?'

He said nothing. He did not even look at her. She might have been intoning Arabic for all the sense she seemed to make.

She joined him in his silence, looking out across the shimmering blackness of the sea.

After a while she thought to pull her hand back but he held on. He turned her hand around, laced his fingers between her own, and helped her to her feet. They walked, hand in hand, along the shore.

CHAPTER 14

SEPEN WOKE TO RUN HIS HAND through the soft sheen of her hair.

'Is it good we go so soon? We can stay in Cox's Bazar.'

'It is good we go.' Maggie had stayed awake through the night, her mind skipping through a whole range of impossible themes. She reached a hand out for Sepen's shoulder. 'I have things to do.'

Her hand passed across the muscles in his back, down his spine, then cupped itself round one of the cheeks of his backside. There she delivered a couple of playful slaps.

'Go on. Get off the bed. Get dressed. We have to buy your ticket. We'll be late.'

He tipped his head back in that laugh of his, put his hands to either side of her, and vaulted to the floor.

She logged the laugh, the swing of his hair, the movement of youth, and watched him tread the concrete floor round the corner to the bathroom.

The water stopped running for Sepen's shower. He padded out, still dripping, a towel wrapped around his waist. His hand swept the hair back from his forehead.

He was posing. For her.

'Do you stay in bed?' he asked. 'Or take a shower? Hurry up. We'll be late.'

She pulled at the tuck in his towel as she passed. It dropped to the floor and she stood in front of him. Reaching to his chest she rubbed circles round his nipples with her palms, then moved her hands down. They slid easily over the sheen of water on his body. Slipping down the curves of his sides she reached beneath him. His balls lay like twin eggs in the nest of her hand. He was still now. His breath came in short spurts and his erection stirred. Other than that he dared not move.

'Come,' she said, relaxing her hold and leading him back to the bed.

'The plane,' he reminded her. 'We must go for the plane.'

'You are young,' she reminded him. 'This needn't take long.'

* * *

The cold jet of water hit Maggie's scalp and her laugh was swallowed in her shout. She gasped some breath back, tipped her head to bubble her smile into the stream, and turned slowly round to let the water bounce off all the new contours of her head.

Then the water was gone. The sound of it was there but the jet arced above her head to hit against the wall.

She looked up.

A wall, lower than the ceiling, was built to form this bathroom within the rest of her living space. Sepen had climbed it. His absurdly young body stretched naked above her, legs splayed either side of the corner, one hand gripping an air vent for support and the other pushing at the shower pipe to angle it high. His hair flopped forward as he laughed, a high and rolling laugh she watched fall from his stomach to fill his chest and spill out of his mouth.

'Are you stuck?' she asked. 'Oh God, you idiot, you're stuck.'

He was spread-eagled above her. She ran from the bathroom to fetch a chair, the wooden chair from the table, and hurried it back in. He was laughing still but his hold on the shower was slipping. The stream ran straight now, smashing onto the seat of the chair till Maggie climbed up and through it.

'Here,' she said, and spread her hands through the water and into the air like she was beseeching some God of thunder. She found his shoulders and held on.

'Back,' she shouted. 'Go back. You'll break your neck, you idiot. I've got hold of you. Don't worry. Go back till you grab hold of the wall again. Back to the top of the wall.'

He did so, she couldn't tell how, while reaching one hand back to push at her head and save her from losing her own balance.

Then he stayed there, squatting on the corner, his back arched and head pressing against the ceiling. Grinning.

'You little devil,' she said. 'You could have had us both killed.'

But he grinned and looked on till she had to laugh. He picked up the laugh and echoed it in his own, spread himself along the top of the wall, then slid down the far side and out of sight.

Maggie stopped laughing. She climbed down from the chair and turned off the shower. He was such a kid.

Thank God, she thought. Thank God love is blind.

'My turn,' Sepen says, walking past her and turning the shower back on. 'You make me sweaty, Miss Maggie.'

Maggie grabbed her towel as she watched him. The towel was dry, thin and coarse. She held it taut by both ends, stretched herself through the pain in her joints, and swept it hard across her skin.

* * *

They hurtled from the runway and into the air, the first flight of Sepen's life.

'Best of all is when there are clouds,' Maggie informed him. 'Clouds look so beautiful lit from above.'

'But this. Look at this,' Sepen reminded her. She had granted him the window seat. Clouds seen from above would have been a momentary wonder. The gift of Bangladesh laid out below him was one that moved him from wonder into awe. This fresh perspective rendered each familiar element of his country new. His eyes watered as he murmured his appreciation. 'It is beautiful. All so beautiful.'

The journey was short, so the plane did not go too high. Sepen could make out the ant-like traffic glinting on the highways. The green carpet of the forest canopy stretched out to bare red mountains. The entire spread of the country's second city, Chittagong, was laid out as a single view, vast tankers made miniature on the banks of its river. The plane banked over the delta that pushed toward Dhaka, water lapping the raised foundations of the high-rise city built on the delta's brink.

Acres of runway were laid across fields inside the perimeter fence of Zia International Airport. This land was too valuable to leave untended in a country of floods and a hundred and twenty-five million people, the most densely populated country on Earth. Men and women were cropping the vegetation with scythes, and wading through ponds.

The couple's luggage was so slight they had stacked it in the overhead lockers and carried it through. Maggie paused in the airport's arrivals hall, and looked through to the figures in the heat outdoors.

Sepen stared too. He recognised people pressed against each other in the heat, waiting to compete for their attention when they stepped outside, but he didn't wave at them. Soldiers guarded the automatic doorways between their world and where he stood now.

'Come along Sepen,' Maggie suggested, and moved toward a bar area. 'Let's have a coffee before we go any further. You need to know my plan.'

* * *

Maggie had given her life to the Indian Ocean, and it had given it back. She was not a swimmer, but she had somehow tumbled her way out into the sea and back again. A woman who could do that could easily bridge whole generation gaps when it came to love. Love could let her cross every cultural boundary in the world. Surely it could.

She didn't need to ask permission. She needed to accept the impossible had already happened. She had to stop herself denying the fact.

Maggie sipped the froth from her cappuccino as denial kept seeping back into her brain. She had a passport. She could step the other side of the international departures gate and Sepen could never follow her. How simple life would be if she made such a move. How much more appropriate.

'You're twenty-one,' she began and looked across the table at her new young love. He was sipping Pepsi Cola from its bottle through a straw. 'I'm sixty. I am a grandmother. My granddaughter is almost your age. The difference in our ages is absurd.'

Sepen stopped sucking up his Pepsi and gazed at her. She was about to wrap up their love story like it was a fairytale then send it to bed. They were together in an airport and she was preparing her goodbye. That's what he was expecting and he wasn't so wrong. Start thinking, start talking, and denial is never far away. Maggie had to be braver than this.

'I'm scared,' she said. The admission surprised her. This was an odd way to be brave.

'I will look after you,' Sepen said. He held his hand over the table for her to reach out and take. 'You will be all right. We will be all right.'

She did take his hand, just to squeeze it for a moment and let go. The squeeze was a thank you for the flush of his self-confidence, for the way he could wrap an impossibility into that 'we'.

'You know why I came to Dhaka, to visit the boy Amar. I still have to do that. I'll call World Vision from the hotel. Hopefully they can arrange a visit for tomorrow. I expect them to give me a package. I asked my granddaughter to post it from England. It contains the ashes of my dead husband. I have to take them to Thailand. I shall let the ashes go when I am there. That will be it, Sepen. That will be end of my marriage. The end of Mrs Mawsby.'

Sepen sat still and watched her face. He understood what she was saying, but he also knew they were only words. He was waiting to hear different words, the ones she was finding hard to say.

'You are scared,' he reminded her.

'It's the city.' She made the reason up as she spoke, but the statement was real enough to pass for a truth. 'That city out there. Your city. Dhaka. It's so big. So full. So different from everything I know myself to be.'

'I will look after you,' he repeated.

'You're good. Very good. But you have your own life here. Some day you can show it to me. Today I'm not ready. We'll take a taxi from here to the Hotel Solub, if that's OK. You can get out there and I'll carry on to the Sheraton. You do what you have to do, see your friends and everything, and we can meet up at my hotel tomorrow. In the afternoon.'

Sepen looked at her, still waiting to understand.

Here's the truth, she might have said, if she could have looked into those soft brown eyes of his and been strong enough to hurt him. This vast yet empty hallway with its pleasant redbrick columns, this café table where we sit alone in an acre of air-conditioning, this suits me. This is fine enough. Tread through those plate glass doors though and I'm in a hellhole. Dhaka's fine for you. You know how to play it. It's the same with me in my corner of England. I'm fine there. At home Maggie Mawsby means something. Here she's a freak. I'm scared of being a freak here, Sepen. Being with you has melted me so much I don't know what I'll be like when I put myself back together. I'm losing all sense of myself. Out in those streets there's only your love for me to hold on to. That's what shapes me. And that you can love me is the craziest thing on earth. Other people out in those streets don't see me and love me. They see me as mean and ridiculous or rich and stupid or something. I don't want that. I don't want to see myself through their eyes. I want to pay my money to the Sheraton and they will tell me who I am. The receptionist will call me Madam, and offer me respect and room service. That's what I need right now. I need it more than love.

But she spoke instead to his eyes.

'I love you, Sepen,' she told them. 'I just need some downtime. Some alone time. Some sleep.'

Maggie's eyes moistened as she looked at him. The unshed tears made his image shimmer. He could have been Italian, she thought, and her stupid thoughts flowed on. I could have flown Alitalia to Bangkok, with a stopover in Rome. Since I was to fall in love so easily I could have done it there. Maggie went to Rome to find herself some love therapy, friends would have said. They'd have smiled and not sneered. I'd have been clever. It would have made sense.

But here I am with Sepen. And Dhaka not Rome is on the other side of airport security.

She blinked her eyes. Sepen came back into clear form. Perfect form. She knew she would not care to alter one atom of him.

'Sepen,' she said. It was a foreign name, filled with meanings for her life she was only just coming to understand. 'Oh Sepen.'

'I will get you a taxi,' he said. He sucked the last of the Pepsi up through its straw till the liquid gurgled, and stood up.

'We can share the taxi.'

'No. I am at the airport. I have friends here. Work here.'

'You don't have to work any more. I'll give you money.'

Sepen took coins out of his pocket and set them on the table, paying for both of their drinks. He checked the bill and put down more. This place was expensive.

'You have your money,' he told her. 'I have my work. It is enough.'

'We'll meet tomorrow.' It wasn't a question, but it wasn't an instruction either. Perhaps it was an offer. Maggie heard the doubt in her own voice.

'If you say so,' Sepen said.

He picked up her case and led the way across the lobby. A rope kept the crowd at bay as they stepped outdoors, but the sun wrapped the slick of diesel fumes around Maggie's body. She kept moving to keep up with Sepen, her breath coming in small gasps. Sepen beckoned across a red Toyota Landcruiser, and helped her into the back seat when it pulled up. She buckled on the seatbelt and turned to mouth her goodbyes through the window. Sepen was gone.

CHAPTER 15

THE PLATE GLASS DOORS OPENED TO SUCK HER IN. The Sheraton had its own climate. The tariff board above the mahogany reception desk showed how expensive its air was to breathe.

They accepted credit cards.

She took the lift, walked the corridor, closed herself into her air-conditioned room, and knew she had found her true home in Bangladesh. As the extractor fan in her bathroom hummed, the neon light buzzed, and the taps purred hot water into her bath, she went back to sit on her mattress. It was firm, yet sprung to yield a little beneath the needs of her body. Trees grew outside her window. The sky no longer burned but was a cool blue beyond the window's tint. She lifted the phone and someone answered.

When the man at reception asked what she wanted she thought of food.

Postcard ...

Flick's next postcard was a black and white one. Maggie had brought it with her from England. It showed a baby sitting on a beach, her grin rimmed by the splat from the ice-cream cone in her hand.

Eating fluffy sandwiches, crusts cut off, in my new room. Cheese, tomato, tuna and chicken. (They don't have ham.) Like feathers in my stomach. They tickle and make me smile.
love,
Maggie

Maggie sat on a sofa in the lobby with her eyes closed.

'Mrs Mawsby?'

She opened them. An unfamiliar man stood in front of her. He curled his grey-socked toes in his sandals.

'I was giving thanks,' she explained.

He smiled, a switched-on smile she was not sure whether to trust. He was in his twenties. Though brown, his skin had the grey of shadow beneath it. His shirt and trousers were of grey nylon. His black hair had curls but they were greasy.

'Thanks to the universe,' she continued. 'For these sandwiches. They're sublime. Please try one.'

Behind her in the lobby a duo was seated on a platform, one playing the sitar and the other a tabla.

'My name is Ricky,' the man said. 'From World Vision.'

She smiled back.

'The driver is outside.'

The plateload of sandwiches in her room was a delight. With this second plate the novelty had worn off. She remembered Saint Thomas Aquinas's dictum that there was no virtue in eating unless one was not hungry. Aquinas was obese. They broke the bones in his body to manoeuvre his corpse down the stairs.

She bundled the sandwiches into two napkins, picked them up, and handed them to Ricky.

'For the driver. In case he's hungry,' she said.

* * *

Hungry or not, the driver was fat. He stowed the sandwiches in the glove compartment and beamed her a broad smile, then spoke as he patted two brown-paper parcels that sat on the front seat.

'They are for you,' Ricky translated. 'They came two days ago.'

Maggie leaned forward to look at them. One was the parcel she had sent herself to save carrying it. It was a little crumpled at the ends but that wouldn't matter. The other came through a special delivery service. She recognised Flick's handwriting on the address label. The green customs declaration sticker read 'Ashes'. The box was ticked that declared it as a gift. Under 'value' Flick had written 'nil'.

Maggie picked up the box and checked it for weight.

It was small but heavy.

* * *

'Does the poverty upset you?' Maggie asked.

Ricky had been priming her along the way, detailing the dire living conditions of some parts of the city and cataloguing its causes.

'You work with these people,' she continued when he didn't answer. 'You work for them. You see the situation they're in. Does it ever seem hopeless? Don't you ever want to cry?'

'Everybody cries sometimes. But nothing is hopeless. We are very poor here. These people are near the beginning, where there is nothing. The beginning is a good place to start.'

'But how do you start?'

'With people like you. You give us money. It buys education, some basic health care. We cannot impose things. Family planning is good, but only when it is your own family you are planning. People must learn things for themselves. Little by little, we help them to do that.'

They travelled along some wide roads, weaving a smooth course between the rickshaws. It gave her space to think. Then they turned off the road and into some tight lanes.

'It looks hopeless to me. What's the point in learning, if you can only learn how bad life is? I've learned, I've studied a little, and I don't see how I can help. What's it like for these people? They'd have to study forever to find a way out of this mess, and how will they ever afford that?'

'I do get upset,' Ricky admitted. 'Visitors come, good people, and they see more than they can take in. They cry, and that upsets me. I do what I can. I warn them, and that's all I can do.'

'I promise not to cry.'

'No, don't do that. Crying can be good. Better than words. It expresses something.'

The way ahead was blocked by the shell of a lorry, its bodywork more rust than metal and the brown engine exposed without its hood.

'Has it just been abandoned there?' Maggie asked.

'No. There's life in that machine yet. They're unloading at the tannery. We're close though. It'll be quicker to walk than have the driver reverse. Is that all right?'

Maggie nodded and opened her door to step outside. The heat closed around her in welcome.

* * *

Maggie was handed a bottle, chilled beads of moisture banding its green glass. She sucked up the 7-Up too fast and spluttered. A nurse was immediately by her side.

'I'm sorry,' Maggie said. 'The bubbles went up my nose. I'm not used to drinking through a straw.'

She had not realised there was a skill to it.

The director of the complex went off, returned with a glass tumbler, and poured her 7-Up out of its bottle.

'Thank you,' Maggie said. 'I'm all right now.'

The nurse went back to the next room, called by the rasping cough of a small child seated on the examination couch. The director returned to his seat on the other side of the desk.

'You're very kind. I'm sorry to be a nuisance.'

He had been making a steeple of his fingers, but feathered them apart and clucked his tongue to dismiss Maggie's notion that she was any trouble. Leaning forward he opened the visitors' book in front of her.

She examined the previous entries, and saw how people had let their comments flow over large segments of a page. The fan on the filing cabinet swept cool air across her forehead several times before she even picked up the pen. These people were doing such good work it seemed pompous for her to write as though she had something to say. It was like she was squashed behind one of the little desks in the classrooms she had just visited. This was her examination.

She wrote her own name, the date, the Mawsby address, then pretended to write a postcard to Flick.

Visiting Amar, though he's not here. This is an office. Lovely sea-blue walls. Sea-blue clinic next door. Amar coughed there yesterday, another child today. Classrooms are white, but children in blue and white and teachers in saris. Teach in shifts. So much learning going on. Walked across playground where Amar does well. Had 7-Up through a straw. People very kind. Off in search of Amar again now.

Love, Maggie.

She shut the book, placed the pen on top of it, and stood to shake the director's hand.

* * *

Maggie read her declaration on the customs slip of the box she had sent to herself. *Football Kit Value: £95*. Ricky asked her for the import tax his organisation had paid on it, and produced a receipt.

She picked up the parcel to carry it down the alleyway to Amar's house. Two young shoe-makers were seated on the ground, in an opening to the left. They looked up and smiled.

'Everybody here works at leather,' Ricky turned back to say. 'These people are Hindus. People believe they are born to their station in life. It is the caste system.'

The people worked at the same trade and lived together. Their houses formed a short terrace. Women gathered at some distance, all facing Maggie, dressed in saris of simple but brightly coloured cotton. A lone lady was standing outside a house at the left of the row.

'This is Amar's mother.'

'I know.' Maggie recognised family touches in the face, the cheekbones, the set of the eyes. Since starting to sponsor the child she had collected three of the annual photographs of the boy, sent with his school reports. 'She is like her son. Hello.'

Maggie set her parcel on the ground. She had practised a gesture in front of the hotel mirror. The family being Hindu she presumed it was appropriate, but in any case it would make as much sense as her English words.

She joined her hands in front of her chest as though in prayer, bowed her head, and smiled.

The group of ladies giggled. Birds nearby chirruped. Maggie was pleased to notice both sounds. She had feared she would be so out of place in this area of tidy slums that all human response would cease, and she would be wheeled about like some alabaster statue. Instead she dropped her hands from her greeting and found she was already relaxing.

'Amar is out,' Ricky explained. 'He went to fetch vegetables but hasn't come back. Maybe he's sitting with his father. His father mends shoes on the streets. People saw you arrive and have run off to fetch the boy. He'll be here soon. And his mother says you are welcome. She asks you to come into her house.'

Ricky and the mother stood at either side of the doorway as she stepped inside.

It was like a step through the looking glass, just one step and everything was reduced in size. For a moment Maggie was a giantess, and imagined a miniature family to fit inside so small a space. The house measured about eight feet by eight feet.

She trod on Ricky's foot, who had followed her inside. He turned her round and sat her on the wooden platform that filled most of the interior. Maggie realised she had stopped breathing. Life in Mawsby was arranged through a series of large rooms. She had had little chance to test herself for claustrophobia. Once she was sitting and could look through the open doorway she tried breathing again. One short gasp and it worked.

'Are you all right?'

She managed a tight-lipped smile.

'It is best you don't take the food or drink if these people offer it to you. We tell them that. It is bad for your health. It is often bad for their health too, but what can they do? They must use the water they have. I could send someone to buy a bottle of soda if you feel you need a drink. Or do you want to go back to the headquarters?'

'No I'm all right, thank you.'

Maggie looked around. The hut was made of boards and patches of woven palm strips. The family's clothes and bedding were folded across strings tied to the walls. The floor space was mostly this emptied wooden platform.

Some light came in over the brick threshold and across the earthen floor. Maggie followed its beam across to the fireplace scraped into the ground.

'This is Amar's little sister.' Ricky introduced the child in the mother's arms. 'Amar has a younger brother, and an older sister too. Another baby is coming.'

Maggie looked at the mother. Indeed her belly was a little swollen. Just a very little.

'Do the other children go to school?' Maggie asked.

Ricky translated the question and reported back the answer.

'The boys are at school. The girl was too old to start. The younger children made fun of her and called her names. She stays at home and helps her mother.'

'Did the mother go to school?'

Again the translation.

'No she did not. She didn't know about education. But now she does and she thinks it is a good thing.'

The lady didn't wait for the translation to end but spoke on. Maggie was surprised to find her so animated. The child tugged at the cloth of the red sari, pulling it back from the head. The mother put her down, adjusted her dress, but didn't falter.

'She is speaking of her life,' Ricky interpreted. 'She is sorry for her home, that it is so small, so bad, that she has nothing to give you. Once they had land, fine land and a house of their own in a village to the north. The harvest failed one year. They signed a piece of paper for a loan to buy seed, paper they couldn't read, and put a mark with their thumbs. It was a contract. Soon their money and their land were gone. They had to leave their house behind and walk away with what they could carry. They had another home in Dhaka, paid their rent, then had to move the next day because the land was needed for building. Now their sons are learning to read and write. They will not be cheated. They can already sign their names. They will be able to keep what is theirs.'

'What will they do when they grow up?' Maggie asked. 'Mend shoes like their father?'

Ricky translated the question loud enough for the lady next door to hear.

'Anything but that!' a shout came back. 'Anything but that.'

The mother's eyes had hardened as she recounted her story. Now they shone again as she let herself laugh.

'She agrees,' Ricky said. 'Let the boys do what they want. Let them have a choice. If they can choose, they will not mend shoes.'

Maggie pulled a package out of her shoulder bag.

'These are just little things,' she said. 'For the mother and her friends. I bought them in Cox's Bazar.'

She unloaded her stock of necklaces, hairslides, bangles and earrings, all made of shells. They were so cheap she had bought a silly amount. Displayed on the bed of her Sheraton hotel room they seemed so tawdry, she was almost ashamed of bringing them to give away.

The lady picked them up and admired each gift from the sea. She looped a thick band of necklaces around her daughter's neck and clipped the slides into her hair before leading her off to model the collection for the neighbours.

* * *

Maggie thought of the golden rule applied by estate agents back in the UK: three things gave value to a home; location, location and location. Move this most poverty-ridden of shacks to the grounds of Mawsby Hall, and would it seem quaint?

It was certainly too small for the two strangers left to sit side by side. She looked for something to talk with Ricky about.

'Is this where they sleep? All six of them on this platform?'

'Seven. When the mother has her next baby. They store their belongings underneath.'

Maggie looked down through the slats of the platform, then up at the ceiling. It was a patchwork of corrugated iron and the sides of a tea-chest. The iron had holes rusted into it. An inner lining of black plastic sheeting spanned the rear half.

'What happens when it rains?'

'They put their belongings on top of the platform, away from any flood. Then they sit and get wet.'

Laughter squealed out from the women in the other houses as Amar's mother did the rounds with her gifts.

'I'll go and look for the boy,' Ricky announced, then left. Two minutes later a boy skidded in through the doorway.

'Hello,' Maggie said.

He raised his hand in salute as he stood to attention. His yellow shirt, short-sleeved and splashed with coloured palm trees, was held together by a single button. He wore beige shorts and his feet were in white sandshoes.

He dropped his salute and held out his hand. Maggie closed it inside her own. A handshake. His hand was tiny, soft and cool.

His mother came in behind him. Amar stepped backwards till he came up against her legs. His head pressed into her stomach and rolled sideways in shyness. His mother stroked his hair and he turned back to look at Maggie.

'The medicine we gave him yesterday certainly worked,' Ricky said. He had come up behind the pair. 'I saw him but he was running. So fast that he could not stop and I could not catch up.'

Ricky spoke to the boy, then translated what he had prompted the boy to say.

'He says thank you for paying for his education and thank you for coming to see him. He can show you his schoolwork. Would you like that?'

Amar climbed onto the platform to walk behind her and pulled his canvas schoolbag down from its nail.

'We give them their bags,' Ricky informed her while the boy prepared himself. 'And their books. And a new uniform every year, which we have made in the projects. There is only one sponsored child in each family, but the other children are given the same things. The baby girl will go to school when she is old enough, if the family is still in the project.'

Amar was ready. He opened his textbook and started to read, running his finger along the Bengali script next to each picture.

At Ricky's suggestion he read from a new book. Maggie laughed when she found she could understand. He paused to smile up at her then continued.

'F,G,H,I.'

He was learning English, reciting her alphabet. At 'M' he tired and fetched out his exercise book to show her his writing.

'What does it mean?' she asked Ricky, pointing to a phrase in Bengali.

'I must be good and kind to family and friends.'

The same motto was copied along several lines to fill the page. Amar chanted it happily.

He brought out his report card next. Ricky pointed out the boy's signature, next to the thumbprint of his mother. Maggie read how he was good at football.

'And are you still good at football?' she asked him. 'Do you play a lot?'

'At playtime,' Ricky translated. 'Sometimes they are allowed to use the school's ball in the playground.'

Maggie went outside to fetch him his parcel.

'You can open it,' she told him. 'It's for you.'

Ricky leaned forward to show him how.

'He doesn't understand,' he explained. 'He never sees anything that is wrapped.'

They untied the knots in the string, peeled off the sticky tape and laid it in strips, pulled back the flaps and spread the brown paper. Amar was getting the hang of it. He pulled at the tab and lifted the cardboard lid of the box.

His eyes grew as round as the football inside.

* * *

Amar stood outside, parading his new football boots and shining in the bright red of his Manchester United football strip. The white leather ball flew like a balloon from his toes. He laughed at the sudden power of kicking with boots and not bare feet.

The ball ran through a rope fence and into a chilli patch, the green leaves marking a small field out of the waste-ground. Ricky stretched beneath the rope to retrieve it.

'This was a settlement until a few weeks ago.' He nodded at the field. 'Houses just like Amar's. Then the owner of the land decided to move into farming. The families were moved out and their homes knocked down. Sponsors sometimes get upset and wonder how we can lose track of a whole family. That's how.'

He kept hold of the ball, then turned to point beyond the field. Another run of houses a hundred yards away stopped by a high embankment.

'People have nowhere to go when they reach here. This is the far south of the city. Do you see that wall?'

Earth piled up some twenty feet high formed a rampart that reached as far around as she could see.

'That's the flood protection bank. If it wasn't there these families would be swept away soon in any case. They're living on the edge.'

He dropped the ball and caught it on his grey-socked toes. Amar chuckled and darted round the man as he tried to retrieve the ball from Ricky's expert dribbling.

Ricky was leading them all back toward the car.

'Time to go,' he said.

He flicked the ball up, bounced it off Amar's head, and dropped it into the boy's hands.

Amar lodged the ball under his left arm and reached out for a final handshake. He caught the edge of Maggie's hand and squeezed it.

'He says goodbye,' Ricky said. 'He thanks you and wants you to come again.'

'Thank you,' she said. 'I am very lucky to know you.'

A crowd of children gathered around the car. Maggie worked her way through them then looked back just before she stooped to climb inside. Amar was already haring off. His new boots kicked up dust as he turned into his home alleyway, running back to his mother.

Maggie looked past Ricky to the children's faces that packed the car window, while the driver inched their car in reverse.

'You're crying,' Ricky noticed.

'Don't worry,' she told him. 'They're happy tears.'

CHAPTER 16

MAGGIE MET SEPEN AS HE WALKED THROUGH the entrance to the hotel and kissed him on both cheeks, careful to disregard the doorman and receptionist who were looking for some explanation of their meeting.

'So glad you could make it. Come with me.'

She led him through to the garden at the rear of the hotel, a mass of tropical greenery and flowers kept lush by a sprinkler system. The hotel pool shimmered blue, thirty metres long and empty.

'A present,' Maggie said, and handed him one of the bags she was carrying.

He pulled out a pair of black Speedo swimming trunks.

'The changing rooms are over there. Here's your ticket. I've signed you in with the attendant as my guest. He'll give you a towel. When you are ready, please come out here and swim for me.'

'You swim too?'

'When I have you to swim for me? I shall sit on this lounger in the shade, drink a martini, and watch you stream through the water. When you are finished, come and sit by me. You will find me very happy.'

He was already wet, freshly showered, when he emerged from the changing rooms. She sipped her martini as he walked to the edge of the pool, smiled for him when he looked at her, and put down her drink to applaud the perfection of his dive. She laughed with him when he completed a length underwater and turned, emerging just in front of her and shaking the droplets from his hair.

'What's it like?'

'Good.' He somersaulted underwater and burst up to face her again. 'Very good. The water is clean. So warm. So smooth. Very good.'

Then he streaked away in the clean movements of the crawl, his body gliding flat across the water.

No worries, Maggie thought. Only happiness. This was life as good as it gets.

On summer days she used to look out through the windows of Mawsby Hall and watch bare-chested young men on the lawns. It was an unsatisfactory pleasure. It left her yearning. Now there was nothing to yearn for. This boy in the pool was hers. She watched him with unashamed delight. And it was good that he swam while she sat for a while. Though she could not always match his youth, she could always enjoy it. It was like owning a kestrel. You could thrill to its flight without needing to fly yourself. It zoomed in and snatched morsels of meat from your hand.

Kestrels. That was another good idea for her plans for Mawsby. Birds of the Empire, eagles and hawks staging displays twice a day. She could costume Sepen and put him in charge.

It was exhilarating, the way her mind was working. She sipped from her drink to celebrate this new idea, and nibbled from her olive as Sepen climbed from the water. The olive drenched in alcohol, a semi-naked Sepen quite darling in his black swimming briefs splashing through the tropical garden towards her, it all registered as a thrill that passed down her spine. Like sap rising, it was the new juiciness of her life.

* * *

Ice crackled in Sepen's glass as she poured his Pepsi.

'To us!' she said, and held her second martini in the air, waiting to clink glasses in a toast.

'No, Miss Maggie.'

'*Miss Maggie*? It's just Maggie now, Sepen.'

'It is not good. I cannot say cheers. I do not like drink.'

'You've only got Pepsi.'

'And you have alcohol.'

'Live and let live, Sepen. I'm not a Moslem. You're not a woman who likes a drink. So it goes.'

'It is not good. What we do is not good.'

'What's happened, Sepen?'

'I talk to my friends. They say it is not good. Drink and sex. It is not right. For Allah it is very bad.'

'Your friends say this?'

'Yes.'

'Then we must find you new friends.'

She put down her glass and looked him in the eye.

'Listen to me, Sepen. Let me tell you what I know about God, about Allah. He made everything in this world. He made me. I can't hide from the world. I am the world. So are you. You're my world, I am yours, everything is ours. I love you. I love being with you. Maybe it is fun for you to be with

198

me too. That's not bad, Sepen. Loving someone, hurting no one, having fun, that's good not bad. It's making the most of the life we've been given. Yesterday you were happy. Then you saw your friends. Look at you now, that silly frown on your face. You have to decide, Sepen. Decide what makes you happy. Have you finished swimming?'

'Yes.'

'Then change. I cannot stand seeing you naked like that if you don't want me to touch you. I don't want you with me if you want to say goodbye. I'm lucky, Sepen. You showed me that life can begin again. If you leave me now, it's not the end. My life will begin yet again. Please, take those bags. There are clothes inside. Your size, I think. Dry yourself, put them on, and come back to me. I won't watch. If you want to say goodbye, just do so. I won't look round.'

She moved from the lounger to a padded chair, picked up her drink, and faced the show of bougainvillea across the other side of the pool.

He picked up the bags and walked away.

She waited and sipped, waited and sipped, till her drink was gone.

The sun dipped behind the surrounding walls and she was in shadow.

'Miss Maggie.'

She wouldn't turn round. She mustn't.

'Maggie,' he tried again.

She was stronger than he knew. Life as a widow was not so bad. She had no responsibilities.

His hand rested on her shoulder. She turned her head to view it, his slender wrist circled by the cuff of the new shirt.

'Hello, Maggie.'

She stood up but did not move toward him. Only looked. The white shirt and the fawn trousers suited him well. The shoes were his old brown ones, but newly shined. He was wearing the new white socks. She had done well. The clothes fitted him. They changed him.

'Are you for real?' she asked him.

She could not guide him all the time. Teach him to fit in, that she could do. But not guide him. He had to live his own life. He had to surprise her, not merely follow.

He held out his hand. She took it, and he pulled her away from the edge of the pool. He took her deep into the shade of a tree and kissed her on the lips. Briefly, gently. Then he stepped back so there were a few feet between them. He held his arms wide.

He wants me to admire him, she thought. Tell him how beautiful he is.

Oh well. That she could do.

Instead, it was Sepen who spoke.

'You look beautiful. It is new, your top and your dress? Blue. Like the sky in the day. It is good for you. A good colour. I am sorry, Maggie. I am wrong. My friends are wrong. It is good. Only good.'

They both stepped forward. Real or not, I'll go where comfort lies, Maggie thought.

They held on to each other. She was pleased to feel the strength in his arms.

* * *

They took their seats in the restaurant. Sepen announced that he would order for them both.

'Are there dialects here in Bangladesh?' Maggie asked him. 'Or does everybody understand everybody else?'

'It is different. A poor person from Cox's Bazar does not understand a poor person from Sylhet. When I am in Dhaka, I speak for Dhaka. Everybody understands me.'

'So I noticed.' She enjoyed watching his command over the waiter. He queried the menu, translated his conversation for her, and settled on their choice of meal with surprising swiftness. Maggie expected to eat well. 'You're quite a chameleon.'

He raised an eyebrow.

'It's like a lizard. A fancy lizard. It changes the colour of its skin to match its background. Always blends in. You look good in those clothes. You act like they belong to you. Like you belong here.'

'I do.'

'I know. I know, but...'

'You are rich. Rich is like a country. If you are in a rich place, it is your place. You think poor people do not belong there. But this is Bangladesh. This hotel is a rich place in my country. I am poor, Maggie, but I belong here.'

'You look very natural. That's all I'm saying. I like sitting with you in this restaurant. You look very right.' Here she was in Bangladesh, being irremediably English. Every word carefully selected to pinpoint someone's place in society. 'I don't want you to change, Sepen. I don't want you to become like me. Heaven forbid. But I do want you to succeed. When I seem stupid, when I am arrogant, practise treating me in different ways. You will meet many Englishwomen if you come to England. If you can handle me, you can handle them.'

'Handle? You mean touch? With my hands?'

'No, I do not.'

There was that fear of course. Her acquaintances who were not shocked by Sepen would very likely desire him. There was fun in having your partner desired, and danger too. She would deal with it in time. If it ever came to that.

'It is a joke. My coming to England is a joke.'

'We can prepare you. You need very expensive clothes. Plain shirts of 100% cotton. Silk ties. Linen suits. Elegant leather shoes. With socks. Maybe no underpants. That can be our secret. Dress yourself in money. Some of the wealthiest people in Britain are Asian. Young Asian men with expensive haircuts. The appearance of wealth breaks through many barriers. So we have to buy you new clothes. We can have things tailor-made in Dhaka. You have tailors and shoe-makers here we can afford. In Britain it is out of the question. So we will take that opportunity. Is that all right?'

'It is funny.'

'Second thing, your accent. It is beautiful. I love your voice and the way it sings its English. It's very charming. But I am afraid it is unacceptable. Most people in England do not speak English. They speak a regional form, with their local accent. An "English" accent is what people speak who rule the world. They teach it at the best universities. The Queen's husband is a foreigner but he speaks it perfectly. It's called "The Queen's English." Your body must wear expensive clothes, and your voice must wear this accent. Say after me: "Oh".'

He repeated the sound while barely moving his mouth.

'No. Open wide and round. Watch. Say it again. Like me, "Oh".'

'Oh.'

He was a very good mimic. He laughed at the odd sound that came out. Maggie laughed too, for the beauty of his young mouth and the speed of the transformation.

'Perfect,' she said. 'And don't worry. You can never sound too ridiculous for the English. You obviously lack formal education, but that doesn't matter. We'll sign you up for a course of one-on-one English tuition at the British Council here in Dhaka. You've learned well on your own so I'm sure you can pick things up. You have a wonderful quality already. You hold silence very well. You are beautiful and move with great grace. You know how to stand and to carry yourself. It's important. You will never need to say a lot. Silence, well maintained, is very impressive. Speak few words but in perfect English with the right accent, and you will do very well. You will meet people, women and men, who judge by appearances. They will test you to see if it is proper for them to speak to you or not. Test you with their eyes, and then their questions. Don't worry. From what I've seen, your natural qualities will shine through.'

'You think I can go to England? With you?'

'If we are to be together, it must be here or there.'

Maggie knew the reality. She knew the immigration authorities in London would squeeze their romance through its bureaucratic wringer. She could keep flying to Dhaka, seeing what layers of permanence time could build onto their relationship. They could discover layers of experience, and learn to trust this history when the present became untenable. But she had enjoyed a drink. She and Sepen were dining in their first truly romantic setting. If she could not give wing to her most playful ideas here, then she never could. Maggie looked into Sepen's eyes and let fly with her dreams.

'You would need a visa. I could marry you, but that would be ridiculous and guarantees nothing these days. You are too young, and I am only just a widow. We could probably buy you a place at a British University. They sell degrees to the really high bidders. But I am not so wealthy, and you are not so educated. I have been imagining another way. I have plans for us. Would you like to hear them? Do you know Disneyland?'

He looked blank.

'Of course you do. Disneyland. Disneyworld. Walt Disney.'

'No, Maggie. I do not understand.'

'Mickey Mouse? Donald Duck?'

Maggie studied his face for comprehension. It seemed she was talking madness.

'You really don't know Walt Disney?'

'No.'

She sighed. The cultural gap between them was so large. It was a chasm.

'He is a writer?' Sepen asked. 'Did he win the Nobel prize, like our Rabrindanath Tagore? Is he like Lalan? Do you know his poetry? His songs? Teach me, Maggie. Sing Walt Disney to me.'

'He is not like Tagore, Sepen. But there are songs. Lots and lots of Disney songs. Let me see...'

Her favourite song came from Pinocchio. *When you wish upon a star*. It was so plaintive and wistful. But in finding a song to sing she turned to *Jungle Book*. Not the film she saw as a child, but the Disney cartoon of many years later. She sang Balou the Bear's song of the simple life; not with the gusto she would have liked because there were others in the restaurant, but still she gave an upbeat performance.

Sepen listened as she sang *The Bare Necessities*, then laughed. That simple appreciative laughter he had, like the boy Mowgli in the film.

'A silly song,' Sepen said. 'A silly song in a funny voice. It is good, Maggie. Sing me again. But not silly. A real song.'

'Silly? You think my song is silly?'

And of course, when she thought of it, it was. Especially silly in a country where the bare necessities existed for so few. She wanted to get Sepen away from there, to place their lives in a context other than poverty. A context of vast and established wealth.

'OK,' she resumed. 'Back to business. You don't know Disneyland. But funfairs? Do you know funfairs?'

Sepen nodded.

'Then let's start there. You have to think of fun, Sepen. I know that's not easy for you, but you have to learn. People in the west want pleasure. They pay for pleasure. We are going to give it to them. Imagine a funfair while I tell you about my home.'

Their meal arrived. Sepen balled the rice and curry between his fingers, helped Maggie to the various sauces, and ate with a steadiness that devoured most of the meal while she talked. She nibbled a little now and again, but enjoyed her tale too much to interrupt it with food.

'There!' she said when she had finished. 'Does that make sense?'

'I think so.'

'You like it.'

'It is strange, Maggie. Very strange.'

She doubted that he had understood at all.

'What's so strange, Sepen? What don't you understand?'

'I tell you what you told me. You eat and listen. You must eat, Maggie. They bring more. I ask them. You listen to your story and tell me what is strange. OK?'

And though her long story was simplified in his telling, she heard that he had its essence.

'There is a big house. Mawsby Hall. A very big house. People pay to look at it. They come because the house is big and old. Because the house is big and old it is expensive and falling down. In Britain there are lots of houses like this. Too many. More people go to the other houses than to Mawsby Hall. They like new things. They like funfairs. Is this right?'

'Perfect so far.'

'But a funfair is no good. The best funfair and the biggest rides in the world, that is OK. But that is at another big house near Mawsby. You want something else. Tell me again, Maggie. That word again. Something park.'

'A Theme Park.'

'Yes. Theme. You want a Theme Park. The theme is Bangladesh.'

'Empire. The British Empire. Bangladesh was part of India then. So it is India. We have a toy train like the train in Darjeeling, going through the hills and the tea plantations. Women in saris picking leaves into baskets. A big tea-house with a wide veranda.'

'Does tea grow in England?'

'We can have plastic bushes.'

'What will the ladies pick?'

'Plastic leaves. At night, when the visitors go, they put them back. It's possible, Sepen. Everything is possible And not just India. Kenya. Aden. Hong Kong. Bermuda. Steel bands. Chinese restaurants. Camel races and camel rides. America too. That was part of the Empire. We'll re-enact the Revolution. The Yankees against the Redcoats. Everybody loves battles.'

'People will come?'

'Busloads. Bus after bus after bus. The British love the past. They think life was good then. They liked ruling the world. The British will come, and the world will come. It is perfect.'

'And me?'

'You come too.'

'Because I am Bengali? I am dark? I go on display?'

'Because you are an expert. You speak the language. You help us with import-export. I can wire my son. He can put together a contract. You get a passport, take the passport and contract to get a visa, and it would be possible to go to England.'

'Import-export?'

'Rickshaws. Visitors go around on rickshaws. Your beautiful painted rickshaws. Isn't it perfect?'

'It is strange. People come in cars and buses and pay to go on rickshaws?'

'Poor things in one country are exotic in other countries. Mawsby is big, Sepen, but our family has no money. We live like we are rich but our house is falling down. We have to sell something to the public, but can't afford anything grand to sell. So we will sell poverty. We will import poverty and sell it for a big profit. It's real, Sepen. It's how the Empire worked. But it is reversed. Before, British people came to India and took all your wealth. Now you can come to England and take the British people's wealth. There will be work for all the Bengalis, the Indians, the Jamaicans, the Chinese, for everybody. It will cause an uproar in the county. It will be a huge success. It's wonderful, Sepen. Simply wonderful.'

'It is silly. Like your song.'

'You are poor, Sepen. You have no experience of money. When you have some, you will see. Things that make money are not silly. You know where to get rickshaws?'

'How many?'

'Start with twelve.'

'I can get twelve. New rickshaws?'

'Why not. Painted brightly. You have lots to do, Sepen. Rickshaws, language classes, export and shipping details, visas and passports. And clothes. Use the ones I just gave you as models to give the tailors. Come to think of it, we'd better get them off you before they get dirty. Let me show you my room.'

'I come with you?'

'I fly south tomorrow. To Thailand. I have to bury my husband there. So tonight we spend together. I want to miss you while I'm gone. I want you to miss me too. Is that all right? You are free tonight?'

'My friends expect me.' He looked solemn. 'I cannot disappoint them.'

Maggie was so shocked she could only blink at him.

He laughed. A full-throated, burbling laugh.

'A joke, Maggie. I joke. See, Sepen has fun. Tonight, no friends. Tonight, only you. It is good, no? Very very good.'

He stood, moved around the table, and held out his arm to escort her from the room.

CHAPTER 17

THE TAXI WAS STATIONARY. Its meter ticked away many of the *bhat* Maggie had just exchanged at Bangkok airport, but she did not mind. She was blocked in heavy traffic, sitting on the white leatherette upholstery of the old Mercedes, gazing out into the heat and fumes and busyness of the streets. Boys walked between the cars hawking cigarettes. They grinned broad white smiles when she shook her head, and skipped on. This place was different to Dhaka. The boys were poor but not desperate. They were taking their first steps in an enterprise culture.

Sepen loved Dhaka. He clung to the outside of buses so full they sprouted young men through their open windows, but he never criticised the poor infrastructure, the lack of a public transport system that would mean more buses. For him it was fine that there was any bus that could speed along wide roads. It was a wonder that miles of these roads were lit by streetlamps at night. It was astonishing that buildings rose through many storeys and that men in uniform stood guard by their plate glass doors. It was wild that large cars with reflective windows nudged their way through rickshaws to move round encamped roundabouts, then spurted forward to disappear in a haze of dust and speed. Dhaka was his metropolis, the sum of all his possibilities. It was as good as a city could be, yet getting better all the time. He was thrilled to live there.

While Sepen saw Dhaka as broad avenues and the brightness of streetlamps by night, Maggie saw it as a maze of narrow lanes through which lives meshed as fluid and threatening as shadows. Sepen saw progress as the city graded slums into roads and heaved up office blocks, while she was amazed at the detritus the progress left behind. The families camped by the roadsides, cooking food scraps over twigs, gazing out through plastic sheets that were the walls of their tents, were mostly farmers. Farmers in a city with nowhere left to farm. She had watched women in their dusty cotton saris, crouched by piles of rock. Rock by rock they pounded away, bare hands wielding metal hammers, turning the rock to gravel, making the aggregate to build the new roads. These were lucky women. They were people who lived off the land, being paid for a day at least to pave it over. Lucky men found the deposit to power a rickshaw over the roads. They were lucky compared to those who had no way to earn that day's food. The world had gone mechanised and left them behind, though it wasn't so simple as that. Mawsby Hall had once employed seventeen gardeners. Now they had one. They had grassed over the walled kitchen garden. They had chopped down the hedges that made the maze, ploughed up the roots and set it all to pasture. Maggie tended the rosebeds herself, to save them from destruction. They could not afford people. The world was losing its beauty.

Dhaka, Bangkok, Mawsby, history, beauty, ugliness, progress, destruction, Sepen, youth, age, love, loss, tiredness, excitement. Maggie's emotions were jumbled by the plane flight south. Sepen had shared her taxi to the airport. She had given him extra for the taxi ride back to the city, and watched him slide the notes into the tight front pocket of his jeans. He held her hand in both of his then stepped back as she pulled away, her hand sliding free. She waved. He waved. He was not going anywhere. She suspected he would wait at the airport, to find someone new like herself. He would smile at them, charm them, and ferry them into his city. Maggie had a return ticket from Bangkok to Dhaka. She had a return date and time. Sepen would be there for her.

Wouldn't he?

And she would come back. She supposed.

The flight from Bangladesh was an escape. Maggie recognised that much as she sat in her taxi, locked inside its air-conditioned bubble. Her and Sepen and the folly of it all. She was running away from inappropriate joy.

Quite right too. She gasped, breathless, somewhat in panic, at how right she was to run. Her and the young man, the toy boy, what a story it would make, if she had a true friend to tell it to. She rubbed the backs of her hands against her eyes, but the air-conditioning left them too dry for tears.

A man on a bicycle, wearing a mask against the fumes, sped past Maggie's window and weaved on through the traffic. She saw no rickshaws here though, just the three-wheeled scooters, the *tuk-tuks*, with their canvas roofs to shield passengers from the weather. The *tuk-tuks* added their puffs of diesel to the air. Maggie felt nostalgic for the cycle rickshaws of Bangladesh. How silly she was to pine for such things. How trivial, how mindless ever to have thought of importing them to Britain for her theme park idea. Some wooden houses still stood between the high-rises of Bangkok, between the building projects. Tropical fronds curved shade around their fronts. She stared into these places of wood and plantlife, as though into some reflective pool. She yearned now for history, not progress. She wanted beauty in paradise. She was a relic.

Her taxi moved, and turned down a side street. Women with long black hair that gleamed and curved around their shoulders stood by the roadside. Their dresses were short, their heels high. Their bodies gained poise as her taxi drew close, and they looked her way. Her taxi parked. She climbed out and the women relaxed. She was a woman. She was not their trade.

The doors of the Orchid Hotel were automatic, and breathed wide in welcome.

* * *

The boy must be new. The cup shook on its saucer as he moved it from the tray to her tablecloth. He fumbled with the silver tongs as he pincered her selections from the tiers of sandwich plates. His white jacket, with its epaulettes and brass buttons, was loose around his neck. Sweat glistened above the plump rounds of his upper lip, the sweat of nerves and concentration. Maggie gathered a finger inside her linen napkin, preparing to reach forward and dab the boy dry, then checked herself. She had set herself the task of reapplying some boundaries to her life. There was no need to force the boy to look her in the eye. No need to subject him to the wash of her empathy. She would pour milk into her cup then wait for the tea to steep. The boy waiter would back away and return to the kitchen. Their lives had crossed to the extent they were supposed to. No more, no less.

She was a widow. She was newly alone. This was her condition, her state of being. Her hair was scraggy. Her clothes were something of a low-grade mess. She must rely on her demeanour. She would act the part of the lady that was truly hers, and not over-reach herself.

Another waiter approached. He was older, in his early twenties, and more confident. He was tall too, and broad-shouldered. He had a swimmer's body. He held himself well.

'Madame?'

He paused by her table. Maggie blinked. She had been staring at him. Gazing more like. Soaking in the aura of his youth.

'Can I help? Do you need something?'

'No thank you,' she said, recollecting herself. The young man spoke English well. His voice was light but strong. 'Everything is fine.'

She smiled quickly, to be polite, then looked down at her plate of miniature sandwiches to break contact. She sensed the small nod of the waiter's head before he moved away.

The sandwich contained cucumber. She had laughed when a girl to learn of the aphrodisiac qualities of cucumber. She clearly needed none of that. She swallowed the corner she had nibbled and set the remainder of the sandwich back on her plate. They had once tried out some Filipino serving staff at Mawsby. The young men looked cute in their uniforms and they were willing, but they looked to be boys with their little noses and tiny hands. She had felt no sexual frisson around them at all. Now it seemed that the presence of any young man could electrify her.

The tea menu on her table made play of the fact that Somerset Maugham had often stayed in the hotel. She supposed his eye for the young men was something like her own. She must adopt something like his show of decorum. The white wooden latticework, the tall thin columns and marble spaciousness, the painted wicker chairs, all gave the hotel a colonial air. Thailand had never been a colony. Maggie could enjoy the place for what it was, without any shred of imperial guilt. The place was a stage set. This was the interval in some grand production. Mrs Mawsby belonged to an earlier Act. Her new character had something wild, something raw about her. She was here in Thailand to rehearse her new self. That was a fine role to play.

She picked up the discarded cucumber sandwich, and swallowed it down without thinking.

* * *

Sepen had opened Chumpers's wardrobe in her bedroom at the Dhaka Sheraton. She called it Chumpers's wardrobe because the ashes of the man lay in their box on a shoe rack at the bottom. Sepen took off his clothes and hung them on the wooden hangars till he was standing naked. It was beautiful to watch. She liked a man to take care of his clothes. The sight of him standing without them was perfection. He pulled his head back in that laugh of his, to shake himself clear of her wonder, then jumped across the room to undress her. He was uncontained. She felt vulnerable before him. Shy, fragile and white. And ultimately, happy.

Now it was back to the old days, Charles and her alone in a room with little to do with each other. She held the Tupperware box of his ashes on the window ledge of her bedroom. The window was open. Outside, beyond the terrace and a strip of garden, the river ran wide and brown. It was a powerful body of water. She saw surges in its surface. Some boats, long and thin and stacked with produce, were pushed by engines against the current. Others sped with the flow. Commuters criss-crossed the water on ferries, stepping out at ramshackle stations where crowds sat at restaurants and cafés. Traffic gridlocked the streets but the river kept Bangkok moving. Her hotel had its own landing. She would travel that way.

Maggie had her plans. She would pay her dead husband some proper respect. He was so much lighter now he was ashes, and the lightness was good. She did not need to play-act grief. However, the spreading of his ashes was a solemn act. She was acting in her official capacity as the dead man's widow. She could manage to dampen her separate enthusiasms for a while. Her guidebook told her of a temple that was reachable by boat direct from her hotel. She would go there in the morning.

As she thought these good thoughts, she was prying loose one corner of the Tupperware lid. Charles's chalked request had been less than specific. *Take me Home.* She had brought him to Thailand. Wasn't this far enough? If she sprinkled him gently from her window, some ashes would surely reach the river. Who would know?

She resealed the plastic tub as she listened to her own question.

Who would know?

She was answerable to herself. That brought the rough with the smooth. She placed the tub in the room's wardrobe. She would find Charles his proper home, before looking for her own.

* * *

Maggie had her own pew in the village church of St. Jude. No plaque or barrier marked it as hers, but nobody else would sit there. If she failed to attend, her absence was given official status. More usually she took Sunday breakfast in bed, read the gossip column in *The Mail on Sunday* to catch up on distant friends, then dressed for church. She attended the service in order to be seen. Charles had not gone with her since their wedding.

'You weren't there,' was all he said when she asked for an explanation. 'There' meant the Burma railway. It meant the Japanese prison camps and the work parties. It meant the edges of death, when disease was the most vital aspect of your friend. It meant being abandoned by all you had ever trusted, and learning to live without trust. That's what she guessed. We live with what we're given. We each have our obligations that we die with in the end. Charles went to war. She stayed at home and went to church.

Wat Po was different somehow. It was Buddhist for one thing, of course, and a temple not a church. Its walls were white, its wooden beams red. English churches had their towers and spires to point up to heaven, but here all the roofs were made of gold to curve and soar like wings. The courtyards were filled with young families, with scampering children, with laughing soldiers and creeping old folk, with a rush of schoolgirls with neckscarves and pleated navy-blue skirts, with monks in their saffron robes. It had tourists too but they were part of the stream. The temple wasn't about death and salvation. That was the difference. The surroundings were a fairground, a playground, not a graveyard. The place was a celebration of life.

Chumpers escaped to Thailand. The thought glimmered for a moment. He was in this country when it was Siam. He was young and in a world turned upside down, and he sensed it. There was something about the country that he loved.

A man stood with a stack of small cages, each made of wood, with bars that were strips of twig. Inside each cage was a bird; small, silent, grey and nameless birds. Pass coins to the man and he gave you a cage. Slip out the peg that held the door in place, open it wide, and the bird could fly free. Maybe you were buying good karma, who knew. It was a cheap stunt. You were paying a birdcatcher to capture more birds. The more you bought the more birds would be snared or netted in the wild. Maggie's Christianity revived at the sight. She felt righteous and marched on. Then eased back to a stroll. It was hard to stay righteous in an easy-going crowd.

People filed around a hall as large as a ballroom. Filling the space, so that pilgrims had to shuffle around the edges of the room, was a recumbent Buddha. Shining gold within the darkness, lying on his side and smiling, he was one more message to counter Maggie's upbringing. He was smiling at the joke that life was effort. She leaned her head back to follow the golden curves of his figure, and the movement stretched a strain down her spine.

'Is it gentle?' Maggie asked. She was in another hall at the temple, this one with no side wall so it was open directly to the courtyard. The place offered massage. What was good for the body was good for the soul, she supposed.

'Yes, gently,' the woman attendant said, and locked Maggie's banknotes inside a tin.

With Sepen Maggie's body became young. It did impossible things. His presence was like an anaesthetic. Some adrenaline rush, some chemical force of love stored up when she was a girl, got released in her system and eased away the aches even as her body seemed to be snapping. Now Sepen was in another country and she ached like hell.

The ceiling of the hall was ochre. How different, she thought, as she lay on a mat on a low wooden platform and looked up. She wondered if an ochre room at Mawsby might be pleasing. Others lay on the platforms around her. How civilised that a temple should offer massage, as against the massage industry that gripped other parts of Bangkok. Her body needed soothing, not exciting.

An attendant came to each of them. Maggie lifted her head to look at the young man who had come to her. He was shorter than she was, shorter than Sepen, but well built. His burgundy T-shirt clung as tight as skin to his broad chest. His forearms bulged. His hair was black and cut close to his scalp. He smiled at her and she noted his almond eyes.

'Relax,' he said. 'Relax.'

She let her head drop back, felt his grip grow firmer on her ankles, and her legs were raised. He lifted them both high into the air.

My God. This couldn't be happening.

'Relax.' The masseur set his hands against her shoulders and pressed her back down on the mat, kneading the tension out of her muscles for a moment. 'No fight, Missie. Relax.'

It was happening. Thai massage treated the body like fresh pasta dough. She was hoisted, she was draped, she was drooped, she was dropped. Her arms were drawn wide like wings, her back was arched, her feet span circles in the air high above her.

She thought of the golden Buddha lying comfortable in his ballroom. As she was flung around the mat, Maggie longed for such a time of deep repose. To rest and sleep in splendour as the world revolved.

'Finish,' the sweet fiend who was her masseur announced. 'Now you go.'

She gave him a tip. It was like paying a fine to be released from prison. And she stood up from the mat as soon as she felt she could.

'New woman!' the masseur announced.

Like the Bride of Frankenstein. Astonished to find she could still walk, Maggie tottered into the daze of sunlight.

* * *

A line of people stood outside a small side-temple. Maggie was in no hurry. She joined them. Incense curled around the open door to greet them. Inside those in front of her laid an offering of money in a metal bowl. Maggie dropped a note inside, to show willing. They had queued to see a monk who sat on a bare wooden chair. He was on a raised platform, beside what she would have called the altar. Those in front of her took it in turn to bow down before him, their hands in front of them, their foreheads touching the ground. This was silly. Those behind pressed her forward so she decided not to make a scene. The monk was a boy. His skin was pale, and marked with teenage spots. His head was shaved, and his eyes large behind black-framed glasses. He looked her in the eyes as she stood before him. Was he a ceremonial monk, she wondered, and any monk in his position would be so revered? Was he extra special in some way, some reincarnate Buddha? He looked on. Her body creaked as she lowered it to the floor. She bobbed her head down, but not to the ground. Kneeling was enough in her own faith. She stood again.

The boy laughed. His voice had broken. It was a high laugh, but clear, and it blew across her like a wind. He handed her a gold cotton thread. Tied to it was a medallion of a Buddha. She wrapped it around her wrist as she left.

A small boy came towards her on the way out. He had a basket in his hand containing coins. She dropped in what coins she had left and was moving on, but the boy took hold of her hand and tugged her back. It seemed she had bought something with her money. The boy ran off, then came back with a small wooden box. It was a cage. He handed it to her and she lifted it to look inside. The small dark eyes of a caged grey bird looked back at her.

The boy spoke words she did not understand, but his hands stretched wide, their fingers stretched out. He was showing her the way to freedom.

Maggie withdrew the wooden peg and opened the door to the cage. The bird stood and shivered for a moment. She turned the cage around, and tilted it up beyond the courtyard, beyond the gold winged roof, and pointed it toward the blue of the sky.

The bird shot upward. Maggie dropped the cage in shock and heard the boy giggle as he picked it up, but she kept her eye on the sky. The bird fluttered its wings till it climbed to be a speck against the blue. Then it was gone.

Postcard...

Flick's postcard from Thailand showed the gilded wings of one of Wat Po's many roofs.

Had massage in this Bangkok temple. Hauled me around table like a rubber doll. I laugh to have survived. So like you did to dead Grandpa. Thanks for mailing him. At station now, taking him back.
love,
Maggie

CHAPTER 18

MAGGIE EXPECTED THE TRAIN to push through tunnels of vegetation. She had thought her journey to Kanchanaburi, the town by the River Kwai, meant penetrating the jungle. The view from her window was verdant but never truly dense. Trees stood in isolated patches, linked by tropical shrubbery, but if she climbed down from the train at any point Maggie was sure she would find a path. The jungle had been cut, the landscape tamed.

Kanchanaburi was a relief. It had a tidy system of streets, many with names in English as well as in the Thai script. Its main roads were simple affairs, not thoroughfares, with low houses and gardens tucked down a network of side lanes. An ancient steam train was mounted on raised land beside the station, in the way that a conqueror might be marked by his statue in other cities. Otherwise the town seemed refreshingly undistinguished. The railway crossed the river here. People and their township were just a consequence of that.

Maggie engaged a rickshaw driver to take her to her hotel. He was a sturdy young man, in off-white jeans and a navy blue shirt. She was in no hurry but the young man seemed to be racing, standing up on the pedals to press down hard on his flipflops. She held tight to the sides of her basket seat as the contraption swayed.

The trip was a mini tour of the town. Maggie tried to let go of her concern at their speed, bumping over the makeshift road surface, and look out to the sides. Here was the war cemetery. She looked through the open gates to the acres of lawn inside. 'We're getting there, Chumpers,' she said to herself. Her case was tucked beneath her seat, pressed in by her feet, but she was carrying the tub of Charles's ashes in a separate bag on her lap.

Some gear clicked in her driver's brain and he decided on a short cut. He spun the handles of his bike to the right, to turn them down a lane that ran alongside the cemetery's wall. The rubber of the tyres scraped along the road for a moment, the rear seat wobbling a dance between its wheels. The driver kicked his right foot down on its pedal, seeking to recover control with a fresh burst of speed. Maggie watched the young man's body tilt to the right. The move was graceful in its way. The rickshaw stopped shaking. The right wheel below her kept spinning, growing extra solid as the weight on it increased, as the left wheel span in the air. The fall to the right was steady, matched by a lurch of fear in Maggie's stomach. She pulled her hands back from the sides of her seat, laid them on the bag on her lap, and gave in. Some falls you can't resist. They are inevitable. You may as well go with them.

The sides of her canopy scraped along the ground. Its canvas roof pressed against her scalp and stopped her flying free. Her legs were drawn up against her chest, the side bars of the canopy pressed against her sides, and she was looking along the dust of the road. All was still.

She was alright, she supposed. Her vision was clear. She could try to move. As she did so, she found herself gasping. It wasn't for pain. She had simply held her breath and stopped breathing. Her head grew dizzy as she panicked for air.

The driver tucked a hand behind her head and took its weight. 'OK?' he asked. 'You OK?'

The concern on his face helped her focus. His right cheek was grazed. She reached up to touch it, but he flinched at the contact.

'Yes, OK,' she said, and shifted herself onto her hands and knees to crawl free. Her limbs all seemed intact. She would ache but nothing was broken. She got to her feet and stared down at her legs. She was wearing an outfit bought in the Orchid Hotel, cream slacks with a loose cream top and jacket. The slacks were smeared with dust. She took a deep breath and looked up to complain.

The driver had lifted the rickshaw back to its wheels. 'OK,' he said. 'Is OK. Get in.'

He patted the seat. The madman was daring to think she would continue her ride.

'Is OK. I go slow. Get you to hotel.' His mouth smiled but his eyes were dull. His right hand shook a little. She looked down to his legs. The cloth was torn away above his right kneecap and blood stained his trouser leg.

'Are you all right?' she asked.

'Yes, OK. Everything OK. Get in.'

He needed the ride, she supposed. Needed the money. He knew the way. He didn't want her help. He wanted her to get back in his rickshaw. The man was an oaf, but he was in shock. She helped him in the only way she could. She climbed back onto her seat.

'Slow,' she said, as though she were in command of the situation. Her case was stowed behind her feet again, the tub with its ashes back on her lap.

She looked over the wall and into the war cemetery as they started out. God knows why she should have had her accident here, with Charles on her lap. The place and timing had an irony she might come to appreciate in time. The driver did go slowly. The danger now was not so much speed as the wheels buckling, for they seemed out of alignment beneath her.

They pulled up at a guesthouse that was not her chosen hotel. She thought to complain but got out instead. It was enough that the journey had ended. She waited for the driver to speak before handing over the money, wondering if he would offer some discount. He didn't.

She gave him a banknote. He clucked his tongue and shook his head in a pantomime of worry. He had no change.

'Oh forget it!' Maggie said. She wanted to get away. 'Keep the change.'

She picked up her bag and walked down the path toward the riverside guesthouse. She had no reservation at her preferred hotel. If this place had a room, it would do.

She paused a few steps down the path and put down her case. The River Kwai swept its broad passage right ahead of her. She breathed it in, sensing the coolness of its passage as it touched her face. Tension eased from her shoulders. She did not smile, but the wryness of the situation had touched her. She had just given a young man a tip for spilling her across the road then bringing her to the wrong destination. Probably, if she searched back through what she had said to him, she would find she had even apologised. How irredeemably English, she thought.

She took a deep breath, picked up her case, and walked on down to the reception.

* * *

Maggie looked at the blank space marked 'Occupation' in the guests' register.

'What do I put here?' she asked.

'Whatever you like,' Malcolm replied. He was Australian. He was too young to be a garden gnome, but would probably grow into the role. His body was small, and for all his ginger hair and beard his face was still too thin. He looked down at the register as a gardener might study a flowerbed, wondering what might come up as flowers and what as weeds. 'So long as it's not "teacher". I'm bored with them. We get so many. What do you do back home?'

'Nothing.' It felt evasive. 'I had a family. I lived in a stately home.'

'Write "matriarch".'

Why not? she decided, and penned it in.

* * *

In the guesthouse next door someone was playing the soundtrack of *The Bridge on the River Kwai*, the tune the soldiers whistled as they marched to work. One end of the reconstructed bridge was visible about a mile downstream. The River Kwai swept past below her.

'Mind if I join you?' Malcolm asked, and sat down at her table. He brought two cups along with the pot of tea. The record next door finished as he poured.

'See the film, did you?' He nodded toward the bridge. '*Bridge on the River Kwai*? It's why everyone comes.'

'And you?'

'Me too. I pretended different at first. South Africa, Korea, Vietnam. They used to send us Aussies out to wars in waves. Men my age just faded into the soil. Now they've stopped sending us. We've got to make our own way. I came here for the war graves. Next stop's Gallipoli, where I'll pay my respects. But after that it's Ireland. The Dingle peninsula. I'm going to walk the beaches of *Ryan's Daughter*. I've been set on it since I saw the movie. So that's it. I'm like everybody else. Running round the film sets of the world. We're all David Lean groupies here. Not that David Lean ever came anywhere near this place. *Bridge Over the River Kwai* was all shot on location in Sri Lanka. But what's it matter? Film's all about illusion after all. We're all willing believers.'

'I saw the film with my husband,' Maggie admitted. 'He helped build the railway.'

'Your husband's dead?'

'Yes.'

'And left you to chase his memories.'

Maggie looked away.

'You're like an Australian yourself,' Malcolm told her. 'One of the old school. Fighting other people's wars.'

'This is hardly a war. Sipping tea in a riverside restaurant.'

The heat had backed off from the air, leaving a pleasant breeze. Maggie slapped her neck and pulled her hand clear to examine the mosquito plastered across the palm.

'Tell me you're not at war,' Malcolm insisted. 'Tell me that poor creature is not a victim.'

'Victim? I'll show you victim.'

She turned her head and waved a finger over the bites on her neck.

'Thirty-two,' she said. 'Thirty-two bites on my neck alone. So don't you victim me. If I could lift my hand and wipe out the whole mosquito race, I'd laugh and wave them goodbye.'

She reached down to swipe an insect off her ankle, then brought her bare feet up to tuck them beneath her on the chair.

'That's how Yoga postures were discovered,' Malcolm told her. 'Yogis tucking their limbs away where the mossies couldn't bite. The itching eased and they found bliss. It was Buddha's trick too. I've seen him do it in statues.'

Maggie smiled and drank some of her tea, then turned her head for the view. The sun was colouring in some wisps of clouds.

'Notice how the little buggers strike at sunset?' Malcolm flattened a mosquito against the tabletop. 'They're here to keep us balanced, I reckon. So we don't get too carried away by the beauty.'

Maggie was reminded of a story.

'A man came to our house once. One of those occasional questing types you find in the military, off on a spiritual journey, treating it as a route march. Glossy grey eyes and

230

brisk in every movement. He was in my husband's regiment, and posted as quartermaster or something to Burma after the war. He told me how both he and a colleague stood looking out over the camp. "It makes you want to give up," the colleague said, and his voice was sad. "We could give them all we have and they'd still starve. There's no hope."

'Our man blinked and tried to see through his colleague's eyes. He looked out over the squalor, at the wasted bodies of Burmese who had come begging for food. Then he looked again at the sun, dipping down over the jungle in a vast orange fireball, coating everything with its soft light. He had been standing in front of human misery, amazed at how perfect the world was. He went back to this vision of bliss.

'I despised that man. I'd have been shamed by a moment like that, but he was proud. People come and people go, he said, but the world endures. He believed he had looked into its essence.'

'He was a soldier. I suppose he had seen a lot of death,' Malcolm suggested. 'He'd have his own perspective. The sun rises, the sun sets. Day and night, happiness and unhappiness, all things are transient, nothing lasts. We have to lose our attachment to everything.'

'You're a Buddhist?' Maggie asked. 'Is that why you came to Thailand?'

Malcolm laughed.

'Is that what I sound like? Sorry. I'm nothing. I just pass on what I hear. A man here has been teaching me Thai, and he throws in his wisdom for nothing.'

'Wisdom for nothing.' Maggie tried out the term for herself.

Her feet were aching. She brought them back down to the floor and stood up, then held on to the railing to tip herself back on her heels. Her arms were locked straight and her face held up towards the sky.

'Oh God, don't let me ever be wise!' she called up.

The tea bubbled up around Malcolm's lips as he drank. He slammed the cup onto the table and choked.

'Don't laugh,' Maggie told him. 'I mean it. We should stagger on to the end of our days, convinced we know nothing. If I were wise I'd never have come to a dump like this. Look what I'd have missed.'

The complex of the guesthouse looked picturesque enough, its cabins arranged in tiers down the bank to where the bottom ones floated on tethered rafts. That was where her own cabin lay. Water pushed its dark and constant mass by the boardwalk outside. The room was basic and bare, the adjoining cabins separated by a sheet of plywood that let through every sound of the neighbours. Water lapped against the pillars beneath the floorboards and shook the bed as it rushed by.

It would be good to bring Sepen here. Good to have him lie on the bed, feel it move, and laugh for her to hear. To lie with the force of the river moving below her, and Sepen on top. Fun to discover a tour of the world's most extraordinary beds that she and he could share.

'I tried not to come to this guesthouse,' she remembered. 'I had a proper hotel marked out in my guidebook. But the rickshaw driver insisted. "You no like, no pay," he said when we got here. Why did he do that? Why was he so sure?'

She liked the place well enough. The restaurant appealed to her, set high on stilts with its roof but no walls, catching the breeze that flowed with the river.

'We pay the best commission in town,' Malcolm explained. 'Fifty per cent of your first night's tariff. It keeps us full and the drivers happy. No one stays long here. They take in the bridge and a graveyard, then move on.'

'They're wrong,' Maggie said. 'It's the place that moves. That body of water. The secret is to stay still.'

She turned her chair to face the river and sat herself back down.

* * *

The bicycle was black, with a crossbar and a basket. The seat was already low, to match Malcolm's height. There were no gears.

'You can borrow it for the day,' he had offered over breakfast.

A woman came out from the building opposite the guest house. She was wearing a charcoal grey dress and her eyes were black, colours to give some definition to the shadows in which she lived. She stood in the sunshine, blinked to gather focus, stared at Malcolm, flicked her hand to throw him the insults she was shouting, and retreated.

'I never use the thing myself,' he explained. 'I keep it for the fun of lending it out. That woman and I have a feud. She also has a business. Hiring out bikes.'

233

'What's the feud about?'

'Nothing. It's just a feud. You have some folk as enemies, some as friends. It's all part of a balanced life.'

Maggie tried to fit the Tupperware box in the wicker basket. It slotted in perfectly.

'A picnic?' Malcolm asked.

'My husband.' Maggie had put on one of her new Bengali costumes with its black pants. It let her leg swing itself over the crossbar with some ease. 'Or what's left of him. I'm going to scatter his ashes.'

'Daisy daisy,' Malcolm remarked.

She adjusted herself in the saddle till she was comfortable, and looked at him.

'It's you,' he explained. 'You and your husband. On a bicycle made for two.'

It was not a funny joke. Literally dry as dust, this was the only way Charles was ever going to share a bicycle with her. Maybe she and Sepen could tour the lanes around Mawsby on a tandem some day soon. That would be something worth singing about.

Malcolm held the handlebars to steady the machine. Then he let go, with a ring of the bicycle bell.

'Go for it, Maggie,' he told her. 'Pedal up a wind.'

She wobbled at first, cranking the pedals round, unsure of her balance, then pressed down harder.

It worked.

The faster she went, the more sure she was of staying on.

* * *

234

There were souvenir stalls, but she wasn't interested in souvenirs. There were the hulks of old steam engines, but she saw little use in a steam engine that rested on concrete. She waited instead for the train that was crossing the bridge.

It came at walking pace, pulled by a diesel engine. A woman travelled in its wake, broad thighs gripping her motorbike as she rode the tracks, blurting her horn to clear the way. She motored off with her shopping bags toward the town.

Maggie was free to cross.

Through the railway tracks she glimpsed the river below. She tried to concentrate on her narrow boardwalk. There were boxed compartments tacked on to the side of the bridge where people stood to allow passers-by. Maggie took the chance to rest in each one, and by the third knew that she would go no further.

She rested the Tupperware box on the bridge's wooden railing, and held her nose to one side as she peeled back the lid. She had smelt it before. The smell of dust and fire had made her sneeze, blowing the first sprinkling of her husband over a Bangkok hotel room. Now she just let her fingers play around inside.

She picked out the shards of bones and dropped them over the edge.

There you go, Chumpers, she thought.

It was as much as she could manage. No prayer, no invocation. Just a tidy getting rid.

This wasn't the real bridge. Not the one in the film. It wasn't even the one built back in 1943. There were two of those. The wooden one splintered to nothing, while this was the steel version rebuilt after the war.

This wasn't the place.

Maggie crumbled into dust what was left of the ashes inside the box, fitted the lid back on the box, and then carried the box in front of her as she trod the bridge back to her bike.

* * *

Maggie had looked through the train window all the way to this town of Kanchanaburi, waiting to enter the jungle. She kept on looking on her rickshaw ride to the guesthouse, and on her cycle ride to the bridge. There were large individual trees, some wooded hills on the far side of the river, but no sense of nature pressing in. Nothing wild. The most she could claim to have spotted were segments of forest.

Now she sat on a tended lawn, for the jungle had been stripped and tamed into soft grass. It ran for acres. There were beds of bright flowers, and single trees that dropped pools of shade. Paths threaded a matrix either side of the central avenue, which passed from the main gates to the far wall where a vast cross was fixed. It was made of white stone, and its central pillar was fashioned as a sword.

Maggie had walked about, up and down the rows of low headstones on this long parade. She visited the fallen soldiers of the Dutch, the Australians, and the British. She read the young men's names, their dates, and their regiments. The stones were marked with inscriptions chosen by relatives back home. Some chose comfort from the Bible. *Greater love hath no man than this, that a man lay down his life for his friends.*

236

Some wrote short poems of their own. Maggie read words addressed to 'Daddy', and to 'the best of sons'.

And then she sat down.

She thought, for a while, of Sepen.

It was not surprising. The fresh-limbed, smiling image of him kept returning to her mind all the time. But as she walked past hundred upon hundred of graves, she realised why he had made this latest appearance. There were many men who died in this jungle without making it to this haven of manicured lawns and rose beds. The thousands of Indian troops who fought alongside the British, and whose young bodies melted into the fabric of this jungle world.

Young men like Sepen.

She shed tears for all the beauty and the years that were lost.

She could not scatter Charles's dust. It wasn't her place to do it. But she slid the lid from beneath the up-ended box, and lifted the box away. The dust settled in a loose heap, a rough approximation of the headstones to either side.

Maggie knelt and closed her eyes. There was no room in her head for prayer. It was filled with the swirl of feelings that were passing above the ground, the thoughts of young men who had lain here for decades and were still straining to understand.

Charles would have no tombstone, but she wanted him to have an inscription like the others. One that could blow away with his dust.

Words came. She didn't say them out loud but tried to picture them instead, as golden letters indented on black marble.

A man had friends
He had a life
He had a wife
Who returned him
To his friends.
Dear Chumpers,
Rest in Peace
love,
Maggie

The neatness of the field reflected gardens of boyhood summers, shimmering into existence like a mirage cast far from home. The tablets of tombstones spilled tiny shadows that would never stretch far.

Maggie ached as she stood. It wasn't enough, but it was all the tribute she could make. To ache in every part of herself, to soak in the sadness from the ground and carry it where these young men could never go.

* * *

She cycled along the river, and stopped at a sign that pointed out the Jeath museum of the war. It was built in a temple compound, the museum housed in a long replica of the bamboo huts of the labour camps.

A monk sold tickets within the open doorway. Maggie bought one, then peered inside.

She could see the glass cases with exhibits from the war; the photographs, newspaper cuttings and drawings on the walls. The hut was gloomy, its smell was musty.

She looked back at the monk.

She liked the brightness of his orange robes. The dark brown eyes that looked up at her through his spectacles. The sunshine that waited for her outside.

She pulled her purse from her shoulderbag, and slid out her photograph of soldiers.

'That's my husband,' she said, and pointed out the young figure of Charles, wasted and bright, linked arm in arm with his friends. 'I've brought him home, but only his ashes. Please have this. His picture. For your museum.'

She smiled, left the photo on the table, and walked outside. She wasn't ready to cycle again yet, but pushed her bike along the road.

* * *

On her bike again, Maggie cycled for the wind of it, out of the town and across a bridge then further along a main road. As she began to tire a tourist coach ahead of her turned left. She followed it down a dirt track. It stopped on dusty ground outside a temple complex. She dismounted, and headed for the long flight of stairs up a hillside that seemed to be the principal attraction.

Dragons' tails formed the handrails to either side of the stairs. She looked down the long run of their coloured scales to the creatures' twin heads at the bottom, then across to the row of parked coaches. Her head span a little, with the sun and exertion as much as the height. Her clothes clung to the sweat of her body. Behind her was the opening of a cave. She retreated into its shade.

A Buddha had its home in the first niche, strips of gold leaf that clung to his body finding life in candlelight. The passageway beyond bubbled out into a series of similar natural chapels, each cave closed in with the silence of its Buddha.

Maggie paused at every threshold, then moved on to the next. She sensed the peace that breathed inside each hollow, but the momentum of the day was still inside her. It pulled her on.

The ceiling dipped and the walls closed in against her sides. She stooped, then lowered herself to her knees. The corridor became a tunnel, and pilgrims pressed close behind her.

She set her hands on the floor and crawled.

The tunnel was long. Dim lamps in grilles above her head lit the roof, but did not show her where she was going.

The wonder of this expedition would be to stand up again, she decided. Her back would then know joy.

She rose slowly when she got the chance. She had breathed in such dampness it would take the sun to dry her out, but only a little daylight trickled in from high above. Electric light conjured the rest of the magic, colours streaking the walls and the domed ceiling that arched back into darkness. The thin cries of bats echoed across the space. Stalactites plunged down from the roof to pierce the wet floor.

So, Maggie thought. I'm in the belly of a mountain.

The womb within the belly.

The symbolic nature of the place, the journey through the birth canal and out into a fresh new life, was suddenly clear to her. Clear too was how much she wanted that new life, how much she wanted to be out once more in the brightness of day.

She stopped looking round and looked for a way out. It stood in the form of an iron ladder. She took hold and reached up, first a hand and then a foot, till her head was in light and the metal rungs grew warm.

A monk at the top took her hand. She held it for a moment, enjoying the cool flesh of his hand. He was a teenager, dressed up in burgundy robes, his eyes a little dazed. They didn't startle her with their depths, as Sepen's eyes did. The monk led her off a few paces, saying nothing, and pointed out the track that led back down. She watched him walk back to the vulva of the mountain's opening and saw a fresh head emerge, then looked for a rock where she could sit and rest.

A crow landed on the branch of a tree below her.

'Caw,' it said.

She sat and shared the bird's view.

* * *

From her mountainside perch she saw a final coach arrive. Two men jumped out before it parked, and the families that followed were in a hurry. They veered left and walked through the temple gates.

She climbed down the track. A teenage boy came out of the gates as she approached them.

'Hello Miss.' He nodded his head above the steeple of his hands.

'Can I go in? Is it allowed?'

'Yes Miss. Floating nun, Miss.'

She smiled and wondered what he could have meant. It was strange how poorly English was spoken in this country. Thailand's ancient history with no invasions had left it self-sufficient. She entered the temple gates and stepped towards the ring of the crowd. They were grouped around what looked like a large wishing well. With a hand and shoulder Maggie insinuated herself to the front.

Cement walls circled a pool of water. In the pool floated the nun.

Her arms were raised above her head, her feet lay straight out in her long white gown, but only the moon of her face floated above the surface. Her stillness rippled like waves to quieten the gathered crowd. She seemed so eternally young, this lady closed in calm, like an Ophelia but for her hair that was not red but as white as Maggie's.

A camera bulb flashed from the crowd, pulling the moment out of time. The nun's legs dropped, her head lifted from the water, and she did a gentle breaststroke to the steps at the side. The crowd applauded, but as the nun climbed out most of the onlookers drifted away.

The nun towelled her face dry. Maggie watched the lines of age being patted back into place, and wondered at the miracle. The woman she witnessed in the pool, seeming so young, was in fact so old. She seemed to have the ability to enter the water and rediscover the girl she once was.

It was an ability Maggie sensed in her own life. She hoped Sepen would get to see the girl who was coming alive inside of her. She suspected he could, at times.

The grace of the nun's movements spoke both of girlhood and age. In her wet gown she sat on the cement rim of the pool. The first of those people waiting in a short line took her place on a wooden chair. The nun faced her and accepted a broad, lit candle from her helper.

The nun lifted the candle to her mouth. She closed her lips around it and bit out the flame. Then she leaned forward. Stroking the head of the girl on the chair, she breathed the candle's smoke across her brow.

Maggie waited in line. The nun's hand was still cool from the water. The warm smoke touched Maggie's forehead, where the warmth gathered for a moment as the smoke breathed into the air.

With her eyes closed tight Maggie saw the darkness of her room in Mawsby Hall. Then it changed into summer light.

She opened her eyes and the nun looked back at her.

We swim in the same pool, words seemed to say, though both women were silent.

Maggie looked away from the eyes, and the head of the nun appeared to shine with a band of white light. She looked back into her eyes, the brown pools of her eyes, and swam for a while in their gaze.

A picture of Mawsby came to Maggie's mind. The memory of the stick in the stream. The knowledge that it was not enough to go with the flow. Not enough simply to float. You have to kick and crawl when the opportunity arises.

Maggie was last in line. The nun and she shared a smile, then both stood up to get on with their lives.

* * *

It was dark and the bike had no lights. Maggie pushed it for the final half mile to the guesthouse and leaned it against the outside wall of her room. Inside she embarked on a current of sleep as deep and dark as the river.

Light seeped through the cracks in the walls as she opened her eyes. Water sounded beneath the raft of her room. There was a knock on the door. Maggie opened it and found Malcolm outside.

'I'm taking the bike away,' he said. He had hooked it over his shoulder to carry it up the steps. 'Thought I'd tell you so you don't think it's stolen. Did you see the bridge?'

'Yes.'

'And your husband? You found where he belonged?'

'Yes. He's gone now.'

'You've done it then. You're free.'

'I'm free.' She reached out to touch his ginger hair. It was glossy in the light. 'You have lovely hair. Do many people come up to you and touch it?'

'Children. I attract children.'

'My hair was long. Children wanted to swing on it. Then I cut it all off.'

'It looks good. It suits you.'

Maggie smiled. She retreated into her room and took the bottle of shampoo out of her suitcase. She hadn't used it for a while. There was so little to wash. She bent her head under the cold tap and worked up a lather.

There was a knock on the door. She opened it. It was Malcolm again, this time with a mug of tea he had brought for her. He laughed to see her.

'You're head's bubbling,' he said. 'Like in a cartoon. They're the bubbles of your thoughts.'

She had nothing to say back, so smiled and walked past him. A raft of slatted boards reached out into the water. She walked up to its edge and sat down. In the middle of the river a floating house was being tugged through the water by a longboat. The house had a roof but no walls and was given over to a party that had maybe been going since the night before. Its coloured lights were feeble in the daytime. Music blasted a war against the natural sounds of the day.

Maggie turned round. Shifting her body so that it was secure on the raft, and gripping hold of the slats, she eased herself back till her neck was over the edge. The water touched the back of her scalp. She leaned back further, till it reached around her head to touch her brow. The dancehouse flipped to upside down, and she closed her eyes. This moment was more about feeling than seeing.

The river tugged at her head. The bubbles of shampoo whirled off on the surface, but she was here for more than a cold rinse. She recalled the braid of her long white hair, carefully draped over Sepen's dark arms. She stayed till the water ran through her, and knew that her hair was long and flowing once more like racing spume near the river's surface.

She lifted her head.

Malcolm watched from a distance, her mug of tea cooling in his hands. He smiled at her ears, sticking out from her cropped head like a lamb's. Beads of water caught in her hair to refract the light. She turned and her hair took shade from the sunlight, turning golden as she walked.

CHAPTER 19

D RESSED LIKE A TANGERINE SUNSET, in an outfit Sepen chose for her in Cox's Bazar, Maggie upgraded to first class so as to be first off the plane. With no luggage to wait for now her husband was scattered over a Thai graveyard, her passport was stamped and she hurried straight through to the arrivals hall.

Sepen was not there.

She dismissed the offers of other men who came towards her, and looked around.

There was no sign of him.

She could take a car to the Sheraton, but there was no point. If Sepen was not here to meet her, then she had nothing else to do in Bangladesh. She may as well stay at the airport and book herself onto the next plane to England.

The glare of sun and dust and traffic waited outside. Doors slid open as she walked towards them, and she stepped outdoors. A crowd was waiting beyond the barrier, hands and voices reaching out, calling for the small suitcase in her hand.

Not again. She could not face it again.

'Maggie!'

She heard the voice, and span around, but could not see him in the crowd.

'Maggie!'

There. A flash of purple. Two men by the barrier were pushed aside and Sepen appeared between them.

She stood still. The crowd was no threat now, their clamour didn't reach her. Life was a tableau, and the colours and sounds, the smells and the heat, the comings and goings at the Zia airport terminal were the blur that was their background. Sepen and Maggie were held at the centre of the world.

He wore his purple shirt with the silver thread. He loved the bright colours. Was it his youth? Did she want to change him? Male birds had the brightest plumage. Primitive warriors painted their bodies and danced around in head-dresses. Male lions were the ones with manes. Yet in her society men's dress was subdued and the women were the ones who got dressed to dazzle.

The top three buttons of his shirt were open. His sleeves were rolled up. His dark skin looked rich against the purple.

Can I be so lucky that a young man in purple waits for me? In her tangerine *shawal kameez*, Maggie moved forward.

'Can I help you, Madame?' Sepen said, and handed out a card from the Hotel Solub. It was an act, a funny game he had planned to amuse her. But the shine of her eyes, her wide grey eyes, made him drop the card. He held on to the barrier and vaulted it, landing steady on his feet with his arms open wide. They closed about her and the lovers embraced.

Army boots sounded heavy on the asphalt and Sepen was pulled away.

'It's OK, officer,' Maggie told the young soldier, his hand on Sepen's shoulder, a semi-automatic at his side. 'We're friends. Good friends.'

The soldier shouted at Sepen, a stream of Bengali even Maggie understood. He wanted Sepen back the other side of the barrier. Maggie took his hand in hers.

'We're going, officer. We're going.'

England was a dream. This was real. Love and fear; the chemistry of both emotions mixed in Maggie.

She followed Sepen around the barrier and into his world.